The Something That Happened in Pepperville

REVISED

PEPPERVILLE STORIES

BOOK ONE

JOANN KEDER

ISBN: 978-1-253270-11-5

Edited by Dayle Wallien and Lizbeth Meredith

Cover Design by Marion Doin

Publisher: Purpleflower Press

Copyright © 2022 by Joann Keder

All rights reserved.

No part of this book may be reproduced in any form or by any electronic or mechanical means, including information storage and retrieval systems, without written permission from the author, except for the use of brief quotations in a book review.

Acknowledgements

It's never enough just to say thank you, but I am saying just that. Ongoing gratitude goes to my thesis advisor, who suffered from terrible mental health challenges while still urging me on. The Keder Readers, my beloved family and dear friends are the solid ground on which I build my dreams. Thank you!

"I am strong because I am weak. I am beautiful because I know my flaws. I am a lover because I am a fighter. I am fearless because I have been afraid. I am wise because I have been foolish. & I can laugh because I've known sadness."
-Anonymous

Foreword

For most of my life, I was a reluctant writer. As a child I wrote stories as Christmas gifts for family members, each story containing a dozen children and a mother-figure wearing big skirts. I didn't think I had what it took to be a "real" writer.

Not Good Enough.

This is a common theme throughout my life.

As a mid-life college student, I finished my bachelor's degree with flying colors, albeit successfully avoiding a real major with a degree in Interdisciplinary Studies. I decided to continue on, aiming for a master's degree. What I really wanted, deep down, was to be a writer.

Not Good Enough.

My master's program in creative writing included several well-established writers. They were all clearly beyond me and some had even made a career as a writer. I looked at them with envy, but knew it was a dream I couldn't fulfill.

Not Good Enough.
To complete this course of study, one must create a novel. For someone such as myself, *Not Good Enough,* this seemed like an impossible task. I didn't allow myself much time imagining and this would take quite a lot of imagining.

We had just come back from a trip out of town, as those who live in rural areas do often, and we stopped for groceries on the way home. In the course of chatting with the checker, I told her all about our trip and how much fun we'd had.

To my surprise, she replied, "someday I'm going to leave town."

It had never occurred to me that someone would spend their entire life within the confines of a city (or town) limits. The wheels in my head started churning. I decided to delve into the latter for my thesis story.

The Something That Happened in Pepperville is about the limitations we place on ourselves. It's often easier to say we can't do something than to admit we won't. Fear can be powerful foe.

Not Good Enough is a phrase (and fear) that I work everyday to overcome. When it came time to give this years-old tale a facelift, I made some changes to make the characters more well-rounded. The message, however, is the same.

Don't live your life ruled by fear.

Characters

Jenna Thompson—local recluse
Donovan Bovant—star wrestler
Chief Blank—local police officer
Anessa Jones—Jenna's only friend
Vivienne-Jenna's mother

I'm having trouble sleeping. It's normal for people of my advanced age I'm told, but my reason for being awake has nothing to do with geriatrics. Never had these problems when my wife was lying by my side. But now, every time I close my eyes, something both wonderful and horrifying happens.

It's wonderful because just as I'm beginning to drift off, I can't wait to see their faces again. It begins bright, hopeful and familiar, like the smell of fresh-baked cookies or the air right after a good rain. Then the horrifying sets in, the part where I remember everything disintegrating.

You'll understand.

Last night, I was on a studio backlot in a tiny neighborhood, protected from the bustle of the movie business by tall thickly branched trees and large, soundproof walls. The twelve identical streets were tidy and paved in concrete, the green lawns a uniform two inches in length.

They were lined with quaint, clapboard houses of varying pastel colors. Each house displayed a shiny red, green or black front door. I walked, in my pajamas, to the pleasant looking red front door of a gray-blue two-story.

I rang the doorbell several times but no one answered. When my dream-induced patience faltered, I turned the doorknob, and to my surprise, it came off in my hand. The door pushed open easily though. My feet stepped over the threshold and onto a bare wood floor, covered in sawdust and littered with rusty nails. An instant *whoosh* of wind caught the sawdust, covering my brown suede slippers and whirling up my pajama legs, puffing them out to clown-size proportions. The force of air continued until it reached my nostrils. I struggled to inhale untainted oxygen, finally collapsing from the fight and hoping in some nonsensical way to find breathable air closer to the ground.

As I exhaled bits of wood, I glanced around me. Through the tornadic energy my weak eyes searched for something recognizable. There were only bushes, barren of fruit or greenery, and a few dead trees. Each clung to the bare ground with exposed roots and some were about to lose their battle against the elements. No faces, no sounds, no trace of humanity. Only the hollow bellowing of a fierce and unforgiving wind.

This caused a loneliness and despair that filled my lungs far quicker than the remnants of wood shavings ever could. I cried out for help, but my screams were in vain. I tried to return to the other side of the door to the safety of my bedroom, but the door itself had been swallowed by the sawdust and everything behind me was disappearing as well.

I reached out to grasp onto something, anything, but instead lost sight of my hands and arms. My slippers flew from my feet and made a revolution about my head before disappearing as well. All that was left was a last, desperate attempt to breathe. Somehow, I felt responsibility for this carnage. This slow and painful death would be my restitution.

I awoke gasping for air, chilled to the bone. I noted that my new suede slippers were now neatly placed on top of my extra pillow beside my head. While retrieving an extra blanket, I looked at the clock: two a.m., per my routine of late. The realization overtook me that it was time to tell my story before it swallowed me whole.

Pepperville

We weren't ready for the storm about it hit us. The day that changed everything. But there's no changing things now.

He lived in a tree overlooking Main Street, in the center of town. He made a wooden shelter for himself for cold or rainy days, but most of the time, Donovan Bovant sat on a branch and observed. Most everyone respected the young man, for something terrible must have sent him to the top of a tree. As a way of showing him just how supportive we were, people called out his name as they walked by every day.

"Mornin' Donovan."

"How's life up high, Donovan?"

"Got the itch to see life from the street, Donovan?"

He was always polite and often waved back, but never uttered a word. That was his way. He was such a part of the scenery that most folks didn't even notice when he was gone.

But I'm getting ahead of myself. How will you understand Donovan if you've never heard the tale of *The Something*? Some of it is fact, some of it word of mouth, and some, just pure speculation—the recipe for all good stories.

There are things that happen in small towns that no one living the city life could imagine. To those of us who've experienced small town living, it's just another Monday. Life here is about dealing with people, not incidents, one problem at a time. The crazy dentist who yells profanities while filling your teeth could be your kid's soccer coach on Saturday. Sending your steak back with the waitress because you found a stray black hair means you may be blessed with another unidentified floating object in your soup next week.

That being said, Pepperville stood out from other small towns, breaching the borders of unique and heading into the territory of downright bizarre. There's no way to comprehend the magnitude of *The Incident* until you've developed a good understanding of the town of Pepperville itself. Strange and oddly fascinating in so many ways, it was like that girl you knew in high school who talked to her invisible friend and only bathed weekly. It always felt as if you should turn and look the other way, but you just couldn't.

It wasn't such an oddity that the cars drove on the wrong side of the road. Heck, the cars drive on the sidewalks in New York, or so I'm told. It wasn't even the fact that dogs and cats roamed the streets in packs of five: two dogs, two cats, and one straggler. (Cat or dog, it didn't matter.)

No, the strangeness of Pepperville was a feeling the minute you reached the city limits. Someone once described my home town as, "a thousand free-floating eyeballs burning into the back of your head." There weren't a lot of warm bodies on the streets on any given day, but you somehow knew they inhabited the place, documenting your every move and registering their approval or disapproval silently.

The air had heaviness like the anticipation of a summer storm. Even when the sky was clear and blue, you could feel the pressure on your chest every time you let out a good breath. It wasn't so much an atmospheric condition as it was just another sensation, because as far as weather went, we didn't have much. The only notable meteorological activity was the wind-it could blow something fierce. A good gusty day forced empty soup cans and plastic bags to dance down the street and into the next town.

Don't be thinking it's all bad. This town has been known for fifty years as a haven for the serious shopaholic. People would drive hundreds of miles to eat a bona-fide chicken fried steak meal in Pepperville. There were candy shops, specialty shoe shops, exotic game shops (stuffed or butchered, one of each) and knickknack stores featuring distinctly unpronounceable grocery items and homemade toys. To this day the tulips still glow a deep, fluorescent red on the hillsides every spring, swallowing the *Welcome Shoppers* sign the city council erected in 1967.

Unfortunately, all of this bounty wasn't available to the expectant consumer every day. Shopkeepers had been known to close up shop on a whim; if the wind blew from the south at fifteen miles per hour or more, for instance.

Fenderson Reekblast, who had inherited *Flowers, Flowers and Fudge* from his grandfather, would lick his finger every day at precisely two minutes after twelve. First, he slicked back the four strands of hair over his otherwise bald head. Then he pointed his barometric digit to the west. Next to the east, south and north, until he determined the approximate wind speed and direction.

One by one, all of the other shopkeepers came to their stoops, awaiting further instruction. Fenderson closed one eye, squinted at his finger, and then either nodded *yes* or shook his head *no* to his fellow shop owners. A nod meant it was time to close up shop. The shoe shop would close, then the *Meat Cleaver*, then the ice cream shop, and so on. It was passed on from door to door, until each store owner had retreated into his or her business and slammed the door shut. The signs turned one at a time: *Closed, Door's Locked, Cerrado, See you Soon!* until all of Main Street was battened down and shuttered for the day. Fenderson waited until all the other businesses had locked and changed their signs before going inside to do the same.

Those anticipating important pieces of mail were

forced to become nocturnal. The mail came in twice weekly to the Pepperville Post Office. Postmistress Charlotte O'Cann had a strong fear of daylight. Her mother once told her that, "No good can come from standing in the sunlight!" and Charlotte believed that to be true.

To combat her fear of daylight, she set out on her rounds at 1:00 a.m. sharp. If a resident needed to sign for a package, she threw rocks at his or her bedroom window until the reluctant recipient came down in tattered pajamas. With bleary eyes the reluctant home-owner made small talk while a cheery Charlotte produced the form requiring signature.

When morning came residents stepped out to greet the sunrise, retrieving their own personal copy of *The Pepperville Daily Times*. They would also find a mailbox full of letters from Grandma, free offers for flower bulbs, and all the bills they dreaded. No one thought it strange. That was just the Pepperville way.

The most interesting resident of Pepperville by far was Jenna Thompson. A small, unassuming presence, she didn't deliver the mail or own a fudge shop. A quiet, auburn-haired string bean of a girl who lived a dull and meaningless existence. I don't mean to be insulting; some things just are what they are.

She certainly was stunning. Since the age of eight Jenna was accustomed to the people she met on the street commenting about her pretty brown eyes and high cheek bones. The abundance of dark hair came to a point just above two severe, bushy brown eyebrows.

That wasn't the end of her admirable traits—her long fingers looked like those of a concert pianist, milky white and perfectly shaped. In other time and places, Jenna would have been sought-after as a model or television personality.

That is if you don't take into consideration her decidedly unfriendly countenance. She never smiled, not even in polite "thank you," or "you're welcome" mode. It's hard to appreciate someone's striking features if she is so shut off from the world that she can't even connect with you over pleasantries. Outside of Pepperville, one with her personality traits (or lack thereof) might be considered rude. Here she was just one of us. There's no misunderstanding her life though; it was as rigid and colorless as the chairs at the Pepperville Public Library.

She had a schedule to her world that everybody knew. Tuesdays, for example, she went to the *Shoppe and Walke* for groceries. The *Shoppe and Walke* wouldn't make much sense to someone from out of town. Customers could ride their bikes into a drive-thru tunnel, ordering from a takeout-style window. As soon as they had all of their groceries, they rode back out. There was nowhere to park outside the *Shoppe and Walke*.

When it was built in 1927, the owner thought cars would ruin the world. He insisted, "No store of his would contribute to the ruin of a good work horse and buggy!"

Never mind that the rest of the world had already

embraced automobiles, and a dirt road was already snaking its way up to the edge of town. When he died, his son kept everything exactly the same, with the exception of the meat freezers he added in 1961 and the cash register in 1972.

Jenna carried her brown burlap sack into the *Shoppe and Walke* at approximately nine fifteen. After purchasing one loaf of bread, one package of pickle and pimento loaf, one half-carton of milk and four bananas, she buttoned up her black polyester- blend coat and trudged down Main Street in her red rain boots. It never rained in Pepperville, but maybe she was more optimistic than we all gave her credit for.

From there she crossed over to Chesapeake, and left at Willowood to her small gray-blue cottage behind the Ashton Mansion, the largest building in Pepperville. Jenna had lived in this cottage for as long as she could remember.

When she entered her home, she left her rain boots beside the door. One day I watched as a ferocious gust caught her door and she stood, waiting. After the wind storm had passed, she slipped them back on and walked up the stone path to the back door of the Mansion, where she found her cleaning supplies.

She had been cleaning the Ashton Mansion since she was eleven and-a-half. Jenna spent hours polishing the fine cherry wood railings leading up the swirling staircases. She dusted the dark oak tables and chairs, and wiping every last particle of dust off every one of the forty-seven mirrors.

Jenna had a real system to it all because the Ashton Mansion had no power and she had to finish before dark, even earlier in the winter. When she finally finished for the day, she ate two slices of pickle and pimento loaf and a banana and then curled up on the smallest, least elaborate couch and slept until morning. At around six a.m., she returned to her small cottage to feed her fish and start her Wednesday routine. The next Tuesday she started the process all over.

It didn't matter how long she was there, at least not to anyone but Jenna because it was completely empty.

After property owner and great philanthropist Margaret Ashton died, her husband's will stipulated that the house go to his eldest son, Drake. All three boys, stubborn and some would say ungrateful, had chosen to live with their mother, the first Mrs. Ashton, in Chicago.

They had come most summers, but other than that refused to stay in Pepperville one minute longer than they were required while the old man was alive. Upon his death and subsequently the death of Drake's step-mother Margaret, Drake did not find the idea of an empty mansion in a backwater town particularly appealing.

Can't say that I blame him, but instead of selling the place he just ignored it. The grand showpiece of Pepperville, an estate that had hosted heads of state and other just as important hoity-toity types, now sat devoid of any real occupants.

Jenna and her mother continued to clean the

mansion, despite the fact that all of the other servants were now employed elsewhere, and there were no Ashtons to look after.

When Jenna's mother died, Jenna continued cleaning out of respect for her mother, at least that was the general consensus. It's probably more accurately described as a habit. It was all Jenna had ever known. She did receive a small stipend from Drake Ashton for her work, a token amount that had been paid to her mother via a check made out to "housekeeping." It was unclear as to whether he understood that a nineteen year-old was now the caretaker, housekeeper and sole resident of the 25,000 square foot estate. To the credit of this remarkable girl, not one inch of the entire estate that had gathered dust nor had any faulty equipment gone unrepaired since she had been cleaning.

None of this would make any kind of sense to an outsider. But those who came to shop didn't stay, and those who were already there, never left. Until the Monday that changed everything.

CHAPTER 2

Some time back, I'm not good with dates

The 1987 STATE WRESTLING CHAMPIONSHIP would be televised on the local station, as it had been for fifteen years. It was the most popular sport in the region and everyone watched to see if they could spot a familiar face.

Peculiar though, people in Pepperville never left town, so the faces grimacing in torturous wrestling holds were all strangers. It was still exciting, and people usually rooted for the boys from nearby Stanswick, wearing red and white stretch leotards that said *Stans* on the back and w*ick* on the front. Most people in the state had a good chuckle about the fact that the letters were too big, and they should have put the *Stans* on the front and the *wick* on the back. No one in Pepperville chuckled. They understood.

Donavan Bovant was one such Stanswick High School participant. He had gone to the state wrestling championships twice before and had won both times, pinning his opponent before the crowd could even glance at the scoreboard and figure out his name. Now that he was a senior, his third win seemed inevitable.

Donavan's aunts, uncles, cousins, brothers and sisters always filled the stands. His mother bought forty-two tickets this year, since Grandma Bovant had recovered from hip surgery and could make the trip without any trouble.

All of the Bovants had the same features: dark red hair, hazel eyes and a smattering of freckles across their cheeks. The Bovant nose was legendary both for its length and distinctive hook at the end. It didn't matter if you weren't born a Bovant; anyone who married into the family eventually developed the same profile.

Donovan himself possessed a slightly shorter but still noticeable proboscis and familiar eyes, but some-time during his early teen years, his hair stubbornly lightened into a honey shade of blond. His parents spoke of his dissimilarity only when cajoled; it was funny to cousins, aunts and uncles.

This phenomenon was of some concern to Donovan himself, as strangers entering the city park on Bovant Family Retreat weekends always assumed he was a guest. A teacher once remarked that it was unnatural for one member of a family so streamlined in features to suddenly find himself sticking out like a sore thumb. The fact that she was a biology teacher and should have understood such matters was of little concern to Donovan. He felt different.

The hopeful champion was a quiet, studious person who took his matches seriously. Donovan took everything seriously, seldom uttering a word unless he had something profound to offer to the conversation.

Grandma Bovant, the matriarch of the clan once proclaimed, "That boy is the blond Jesus. He's the second coming, I'm telling you..."

No one disagreed.

Perhaps this contributed to his eventual downfall? That's quite the moniker to hoist on the shoulders of a teen boy. I could speculate, but it's really just that, speculation.

Donovan's four brothers were allowed leave from the meat packing plant for the state wrestling event. No other activity, sporting or otherwise was momentous enough for approved time off, and two solid days at that. But the plant manager was a second-cousin-once removed to the Bovant family.

He shared the same dark red hair and now-faded freckles, along with a passion for public showings of family unity. He insisted that all employees have access to a television during Donovan's matches. The noisy grinders were turned off for almost thirty minutes at a time. Those who didn't re-live their youths through the Bovant family sporting events still relished the extra breaks.

It was more than a complete shut-down of hamburger grinding for this seemingly normal neighbor to Pepperville. More people in Stanswick watched the local boys competing than watched the last presidential inauguration. Even school children were allowed time out from lectures and books to see the shining stars compete from high schools all across the state.

Since Stanswick contained no more than 400 souls, a good portion of the city was seated in the State Fair Gymnasium to watch the matches. The untimely demise of those in the gym would have meant an abrupt end to the entire city council, school board, dentistry and pastoral portion of the village.

Now that Donovan was representing Stanswick at the state level, his future looked bright. There was certain to be a wrestling scholarship waiting for him at the end of his senior year. His father, two uncles and a grandfather had been prior recipients and had all attended Iowa State University solely based on their wrestling abilities. For the first time in family history, a Bovant would attend college in possession of mental acuity as well. For the first time in Stanswick High School history, a Bovant had actually earned the exceptional marks given to him.

The arrival at the Des Moines Holiday Inn was uneventful. The subsequent team swim party included all bus riders, with the exception of Donovan. He sat in a plastic deck chair and did not even remove his shoes. He chose not to acknowledge the playful splashes of his team mates, and turned his head in the other direction when his name was called. They had become accustomed to his aloof nature, so unlike the boisterous temperament of the rest of his family.

Donovan wasn't the only representative from Stanswick in Des Moines. Fred Baily, John Moran, and Luke Wright also made the trip. Fred lost his match in a heartbreaking pin last year, but John and Luke were competing for the first time. Neither had family members attending, so Donovan's large contingent promised to cheer for the other boys as well.

By the time the huge Bovant family arrived at the Airport Snooze Inn, the wrestling team was already in the State Fair gymnasium, warming up for their preliminary matches. There were four rounds of elimination, the first three occurring in one day. Six brightly colored, rubber wrestling mats lined the floor from end to end, covering the newly re-stained hardwood. The circle painted in the center of each mat said *STATE FAIR*

After mandatory stretching, each team member retreated to his own state of mind. There were many theories on mental preparation, each encouraged by a coach at one point or another in a boy's wrestling career. Some boys pictured a scene of parental rebuking to fire themselves up: *Get that damn room cleaned up! I thought I told you never to bring girls into this house! One more time I catch you with booze, and you are out on your ass!*

Others needed serene and gentle reassurance to balance their minds. *Breathe deeply. Think of calming ocean waves. You are in a quiet and peaceful state of being.* Some just sat and pretended to concentrate while checking out the cheerleaders from neighboring towns. When the loudspeaker announced the National Anthem, athletes and spectators alike snapped to attention. A cheerleader from Beamon High sang all the words she remembered. It was time for the first round to begin.

The Bovants, meanwhile were busy demanding extra ice buckets and hypo-allergenic pillows. There was no need to watch the preliminary rounds on public television, a Bovant never lost those.

Most of the adults were heavy drinkers, and most of the children were highly allergic to down-bedding of any sort. When all were settled in, they traveled en mass to the *Country Clucker* across the street where they cleaned out the State's Biggest Buffet (or so the sign said) in a matter of minutes.

The family feasted on buffet-style chicken fried steak and cold spaghetti and retired poolside with Jim Beam Whiskey and Amaretto laced with milk. The young ones honed their swim-suit snapping and water farting skills.

Leona Bovant found the closest parking spot she could. She was a massive, "big-boned" woman, but normally quite physically fit. The new hip had set her back a bit though, and she didn't want to waste time trying to prove she was capable of walking three blocks when she knew that she wasn't.

By two o'clock, everyone piled into the stadium to watch Donovan in his second match. As Leona rounded the building and entered through the gym doors, she thought about how proud her grandchildren had made her. So much more so than her own children. Each had excelled at something.

Little Limona Jean was the family songstress, winning the Moose Lodge Talent Show three years in a row. Jackie experimented with all sorts of unusual ingredients and usually won the First Prize ribbon at the county fair for one concoction or another. And those boys—every darn one of them was a wrestling superstar. Now she had the Grandma Supreme, a grandson with smarts as well as excelling in sports. She grinned to herself.

After showing her ticket and getting the STAWRES stamp on her hand, in case she wanted to leave and then re-enter, (state wrestling was just too long for the stamper) she searched for the rest of her brood.

"Grandma Bovant!" someone called from the crowd. Leona turned and waved. She reveled in her popularity. She was as well-known as her wrestling grandsons at these events.

"Well now that Grandma's here, we can git some serious wrastlin' done," A pot-bellied man in the front row hollered.

"Oh, you behave now Delbert Rucksford," Leona teased.

She glanced around the stand and finally found the concentration of red-heads and GO DONOVAN banners clear at the top on the opposite end of the gym.

One of her granddaughters stood waved. She had saved Grandma a seat on the end so that Leona wouldn't have to navigate the narrow benches lined with impatient parents. She did have a new hip to deal with, after all.

"'Nother Bovant at the top. "Someone commented. Grandma slowed her gait and her limp became more prominent as she crossed in front of a large group of Stanswick supporters.

As she found her seat, she removed her jacket to display a maroon sweatshirt she made herself. With gold fabric paint she painstakingly decorated the words, STANSWICK GRANDMA on the front and WE WRASSEL on the back. From her oversized purse she removed a plastic cushion that said STANSWICK RASCALS and placed it gingerly under her new hip. She gave a simple nod to Donovan's mother, who was her least-favorite daughter-in-law.

Grandma Bovant, now settled, waited patiently for her grandson to win his state title.

CHAPTER 3

Exercise, Pepperville style

That week had been extraordinarily dull. No wind, no out of town customers, not even a crime to speak of, unless you counted the theft of four issues of the *Pepperville Daily Times* (delivered thrice weekly) from the machine in front of the *Shoppe and Walke*.

This kind of thievery only took place when Emily Wigworth, *Pepperville Daily Times* editor, placed a picture of someone's adorable progeny on the front page. (Locals had to have something to share with the relatives, even if they were out of change.) Chief Blank promised he would investigate soon.

And speaking of the paper, Emily knew that some people would skim over the paper and only read the front page news before heading off to work. That's why she printed the paper backwards, with page eight coming first. It was just as important, she reasoned, to read about Mrs. McCorkle finding a Woolly

Mammoth tooth in her backyard as it was to hear what the City Council had decided to do about filling the enormous potholes.

So page eight *Gossip Spot* came first, then seven, page six with its lengthy obituaries and detailed police record, the sports on page five, and by the time you reached the front page news (printed on the last page but titled *Front Page*) you knew every bit of important information in the entire town of Pepperville. It didn't make sense that it was called the *Daily Times* when it came three times a week. But that was Pepperville.

Today was Jenna's semi-annual closet cleaning. She chose a different Ashton bedroom each time to clean and today in the Buttercup room, she discovered a pile of old newspapers.

Page Eight featured a new exercise studio that caught Jenna's attention. After the death of her mother, she had forced herself to leave the house regularly to walk or jog, simply because it cleared her head. But in time she realized she needed more. The ad, placed two years ago this November, read:

Are you ready for a change? Get up and move with us! Friendship and fabulous abs included!

Join us at Calley Sthenics Aerobic Studio

-Calley Walker, owner and exercise instructor

She could exercise and socialize, without actually speaking. Jenna decided it was worth a try.

Calley Walker was just short of fifty years old, or so everyone thought. Frequently she mentioned an approaching birthday but the exact date was always unclear. Lucky for her, she didn't look a day over thirty. Thanks to Calley's exuberant personality and creative classes, women could sweat and nod and Calley would do the rest.

Calley was thought to be quite worldly. She had a cousin who lived in Stanswick, and they spoke frequently. She sent Calley her old exercise videos, and told Calley they were the latest in exercise technology. She never mentioned the fact that she had been trying to sell them at garage sales for five years without success. Calley liked to blend her own unique ideas with the information she gained from the videos for a truly specialized workout.

The first class was a big step for Jenna. She stood outside the building for twenty minutes. When she entered mid class, Calley walked over and put her arm around Jenna.

"And kick those legs...kick, kick, kick..." She continued to exercise as she took Jenna's shoulders and guided her to the empty spot in the back.

Jenna was grateful, both for the lack of formal introduction and the place at the back of the room.

After attending five classes, Jenna finally felt at ease both in Calley's presence as well as the other women.

Today's class was Sculpting-On-The-Go. Calley waved to Jenna as she stepped inside the studio.

"Hey Girl," Calley called. (A term she had learned from the lively banter in *Aerobics for Y'all, 1980.*) "Come on in!"

Jenna nodded as she slipped off her coat. She fell in

line behind Calley's daughter, Jane and followed the group as they paraded around the gym, lifting their knees high in the air and squeezing their palms together in front of their chests.

"We'll squeeze, we'll heave, until our chests do cleave!" They chanted.

Calley herself was quite small busted, but assured the class it was the result of too much dairy, not her knowledge of physical activity. (*Build a Better Bust With Buddy, 1982*)

What this middle-age woman lacked in knowledge she made up for with her youthful exuberance. The nursing home looked forward to her Sunday afternoon visits. The grade schoolers squealed with joy when she made surprise appearances in their P.E. classes. Her bright brown eyes lit up at the sight of any potential sheep joining her flock of aerobic lambs.

Jenna decided this wasn't so bad, and that maybe she could squeeze Calley s'thenics into her regular schedule.

Calley's gray-streaked hair sparkled with sweat as she paraded one last time around the room. "OK, girls that's enough of that. I want to show you something new I learned this week." The women wiped their brows with the burnt orange hand towels provided for them.

"I want to show you how to crunch. Now I know ya'll think I'm talking about food. But this is more for your inner belly. "She lay down on the floor and began to demonstrate the half sit-up found on *No More Flab on the Ab.* "Just like this, ladies."

Her push to pseudo sit-up revealed two distinctive folds of skin on either side of her black spandex belt. Instead of stopping with the simple procedure she had learned on the video, she improvised, as usual, another step.

As she held the back of her head and started to rise, she made a "froooooo" reverberation with her lips. When her head almost touched her knees, she made a new sound, a sort of "Ya'AHH!" sound. She sat up and glanced around the room. The women sat up slowly and waited for further instruction.

Calley pushed a long gray strand of hair behind her ear and smiled with satisfaction.

"Ya'll see what I mean? It's that little kick at the end that makes your tummy oh- sooo tight!" Twenty-five heads nodded in agreement. They all laid down on their homemade cloth mats and began the Calley Crunch. Twenty-five heads rose at the end and proclaimed, "Ya 'AHHH!" in unison. It was a beautiful sight.

After thirty more minutes of toning and conditioning, it was time for Friendly Food and Folly. (FFAF), Calley's idea for post-workout socialization. Jenna, who had assigned herself the role of hostess, plugged in the coffee pot during cool down after each class.

She prided herself on her coffee creations and served a different flavor after every class. A little bit of several different instant coffees mixed together made quite the flavor sensation. This week her mouth-watering blend was entitled, *Vanilla Ice Cream, and Banana Flambe Decaf.* After the Styrofoam cups were stacked twenty-five high, she opened the small white refrigerator to see what new healthy treat Calley had provided. Her eyes scanned the shelves of neatly organized and labeled plastic containers until she found one marked, *FFAF, Friday.*

Jenna sat the container on the counter and slowly opened the lid in a defensive mode, as if something were about to jump out and attack her. The brownish bars were a combination of oats, wheat germ, raisins, dates and if she wasn't mistaken, a fossil fuel.

When the smell hit her nostrils, she fought the urge to cry out in disgust. Her lips pressed tightly together, she didn't utter a single sound. Instead, she turned her attention to the cool-down taking place in the main room.

".......ssssheeeeee...breathe out, girls."

Jenna closed the door to the kitchen/broom closet and began her weekly routine.

As secrets go, some are worse than others. By Pepperville standards, this one was minute. Jenna stood on her tip toes, opening a small door that was supposed to house cleaning supplies. Instead, there were rows and rows of contraband edibles—frostings, cake mixes, lard and sugar. She moved the white sugar aside and was just barely able to reach the crystallized brown sugar in the back. After sprinkling the bars liberally, she took a spatula and pressed the sugar bits into the bars so that they looked as if they were baked in from the beginning. Almost anything Calley baked could be repaired with sugar.

Though she'd just begun exercise class recently, Jenna had been cleaning for Calley since she was in the sixth grade, initially at the encouragement of her mother. Something that began as a way to earn extra cash had now become a more vital part of her existence: A reason to be somewhere other than the Ashton property where the quiet and her singular existence often engulfed her.

Calley gave her fifteen dollars every week and didn't ask how much of that was spent on the products she used. It was only after a debacle of prune and pineapple-carob cookies that she discovered her calling.

The day of the prune bars, when the class simultaneously grimaced at first bite, Jenna assured them that Calley hadn't been given the correct recipe. She couldn't let them discover Calley's weakness- how would they continue to trust her exercise leadership? It was Jenna's duty to make sure her classmates (the bi-weekly outing she most looked forward to) had sufficient snacks.

"Ahhh... now pull the other leg straight up....ahh. Ya'll have done great! See you on Thursday!"

Jenna pushed the last of the sugar bits into the container and quickly hid her tool of deception. She met Calley at the door. "Just in time! These look wonderful, Calley! What do you call them?"

She raised her dark eyebrows, trying to feign interest.

Calley smiled with pride. "Ya'll can call them whatever you want. They are somethin' healthy I found in a magazine. There's not one ounce of sugar. Purified raisins are the key ingredient this week, so enjoy!"

Not one voice piped up to ask exactly what a purified raisin was. Each member took a bar and poured herself a cup of coffee.

"So Jenna, you watchin' wrestlin' this weekend?" Calley asked.

"Umm....no, I have other things to do."

Jenna looked away; she was a terrible liar.

Calley shook her head. "Ya' know girl, you need to get out. Make some friends. Maybe ask someone over to watch with you."

The exercise queen of Pepperville had taken on a motherly air since the death of Jenna's mother, much to Jenna's chagrin. She felt a little resentful that Calley tried to take her mother's place.

Jenna restacked the cups, the color rising in her cheeks. "There's some maintenance that needs done around the Ashton place. Outdoor stuff while it's still nice."

"Part of good physical well-being is good mental well-being. I'm gonna challenge you... to challenge you!"(*Challenge your body, Challenge your soul, 1979*) Calley poked a bright pink fingernail into Jenna's chest. "Call someone and ask them to come over tomorrow and I'll stop buggin' you about finding a date."

Jenna shrunk from her touch, and her suggestion. She lacked the enthusiasm for any relationship, let alone one with an actual date.

"I don't even know how to have a sports party." Jenna replied.

Secrets were a popular commodity in Pepperville but privacy wasn't, and the word "party" instantly evoked excitement from this particular group. Several women now joined in the conversation, giving Jenna unsolicited advice on hostessing an event of such magnitude.

"Pre-printed invitations are a must."

"You need some socialization dear. Otherwise, you'll start talking to yourself, and then you'll start seeing things that aren't there. It might have already begun."

"You'll need matching napkins."

"Make sure you offer your guest plenty of beverages."

"Take a cleansin' breath, ladies. (*Breathe In, Breathe Out, 1984*) She's havin' a friend over, not hostin' a school board meeting," Callie cautioned. She pivoted toward Jenna. "I'll help you find someone," she said reassuringly. "It ain't a big deal."

Callie cocked her head to the side, trying to read the clock in the other room without squinting. "Ffaf's done for today! I got yoga in an hour!"

"I hate wrestling." Jenna groaned weakly.

An opportunity to chat with a friend and watch wrestling on a Saturday morning seemed harmless enough; at least it would have to me. Jenna certainly could have no way of knowing the decision to turn on her television set would change the course of her life. But then, this wasn't the first time that a last minute change-of-heart had caused far-reaching consequences in Pepperville.

One day after twenty-some years of turning left on the street behind the high school, the principal of Pepperville Eight Thru Twelve decided to turn right. He told his golfing buddies later that the only reason he turned right was to look at the new shade of cream his secretary had used to paint her patio. The rumor mill though, which was accurate more times than not, circulated a story about his interest in a certain postmaster who slept in the nude during the day with all four window shades up.

In any event, that right hand turn took two playful squirrels by surprise. They jumped and scampered away at the sound of his car. In an attempt to swerve and avoid the squirrels, the unsuspecting principal swerved up on the curb and into the lawn of the Rupert family, where four year-old Eugenia Rupert lay, quietly staring at the cloud formations.

She often snuck out onto the front lawn during naptime, her mother later reported, and since people rarely drove down her block and her daughter usually fell asleep while observing the clouds, "bunny tales" as she called them, Eugenia's mother never saw the harm in it.

Although the details were reported at the end of the week in the *Pepperville Daily Times*, there is really no need to repeat them. Suffice to say there was little left of Eugenia after her encounter with the heavy body of the Chrysler sedan.

Eugenia's devastated family moved to another block, one hidden from known streets and without easy access from a main road. The principal bought the Rupert house as his own self-imposed punishment and lived in the dark basement for the few years of life he had left.

A tortured man, or as was whispered at the coffee shop, "an old guy who's not right in the head," he aged to the appearance of an elderly man, pained by each step he took instead of the forty-seven year old educator who existed before the fateful right turn.

Jenna's ostensibly easy decision to watch television did not cause a catastrophic event like the death of a child. No one lost his life as a result of the click of a button in her living room, but the chain of events set into motion were certainly just as dramatic and the results would be felt for many years to come.

CHAPTER 4

Anessa

nessa Prembone arrived in the middle of exercise class, after late shift at the *Shoppe and Walke* had ended. From the window, she peered at her reflection's touching both of her eyelids. She wanted to make sure she'd remembered to apply a thick coat of her trademark, Azure Sparkle eye shadow.

Even though she was late, Anessa Prembone always made sure she looked her best.

She realized she was only marginally attractive. Her blonde bangs were cut in a straight line slightly above her eyebrows and the rest of her hair, bleached in the spots Anessa could reach with Sun In bleach, (meant to emulate a sun-kissed color) was shorn two inches below her ears. The straight strands tucked against her face in a decidedly unattractive way.

Anessa turned from one side to the other, admiring what she saw. She insisted upon wearing a leotard to class, one that made her ample body look like a thick, Italian sausage stuffed into the casing of a more aesthetically pleasing breakfast sausage.

I'm not saying that to be cruel. She was one of those people whose smile lit up her face and everyone else's in the room. When she wore makeup to cover her acne scars, her face almost glowed.

Long ago she gave up her glasses and rarely wore her prescribed contact lenses. Her brother Greg informed that he read contact lenses would someday make her cross-eyed. This led to some embarrassing moments when Anessa couldn't read the price of a grocery item, and just guessed at its approximate value when charging the customer. There was a run on mayonnaise the day she charged one customer thirty-five cents for an economy-sized jar.

Her eyes scanned the group until she found Jenna pouring coffee. The two were the only twenty-some-things attending the class, and by default had formed a friendship.

Calley pulled her aside before she could reach Jenna. "Ya'll need somethin' to do this weekend?" she asked.

Anessa eyed her suspiciously. The last time a conversation began this way, Anessa spent the weekend cleaning Calley's gutters. Anessa assumed it had been more of a social invitation, and had come dressed in her most expensive pair of blue jeans and a knee-length sweater her mother knitted for her from multi-colored yarn.

"Um—I was gonna watch wrestling."

"Perfect! Go ask Jenna!" Calley replied with her usual enthusiasm. "And don't ya'll take no for an answer."

Anessa's face lit up. Jenna was an enigma, a woman of mystery. No one in Pepperville had spent any length of time with her and such an invitation would improve Anessa's social standing. Despite what she perceived as a growing friendship between them, Jenna had yet to agree to them spending time together outside of class.

She immediately made a beeline to the other side of the room.

"Hey! Sorry I was late. Five people came through my line just when it was time for me to punch out!" Anessa touched Jenna's shoulder warmly.

Jenna jumped at the unexpected human contact and then wrapped her arms around her scant waist, as if that were what she was planning all along.

"Jenna, do you want to come over and watch the State Wrestling thingy with me this weekend? We can pick out the guys we think are hot." Anessa asked, grabbing three bars and immediately stuffing one in her mouth.

Jenna shrugged her shoulders. "I'm two years out of high school. Don't think I want to stare at high school boys. Why do you?"

"You never do anything, Jenna. Remember when that new game show was on, and my tv was on the blink?" crumbs tumbled from Anessa's mouth, but she didn't seem to notice.

Jenna sighed.

"I know. I was supposed to make brownies with you, but I got a headache."

Anessa's jaw dropped. "You said you were in the middle of a Russian history book. Did you lie to me?"

Jenna rubbed the back of her neck, frowning. "How do you remember these things?"

"I get it. I'm too energetic for you and you don't like it that I'm always searching for that perfect guy."

A look of relief crossed Jenna's face. "Yeah, something like that."

"Well, this time I'm not accepting no for an answer. You're coming over and that's that. I promise I'll be calm and won't talk about guys."

Anessa shot Calley a not-so-subtle thumbs up and a nod.

"You know, Anessa, men don't care for women who were always so...available. That's what my mother used to say."

Jenna bit her lip and turned away.

"Your mother only left the mansion to run errands for the Ashton family. I doubt she had any experience with men, outside of your mysterious father," Anessa retorted. When she noticed Jenna's face was beat red, she grabbed her friend's arm and pulled her in close.

"I didn't mean that. I know it's a big secret, even from you. I'd never say anything–"

Jenna pushed her away. "Ok, I'll come over for an hour or two. But then I really need to get back home. I have responsibilities at the mansion. That hardly leaves me time for...things."

Anessa released Jenna from her grip and smiled broadly, exposing one crooked tooth. "Let's do it at your place, so you don't have to be in a hurry. I'll bring pizza "

She pivoted once more and winked at Calley, who gave her a "thumbs up."

Meeting at Jenna's place had an added bonus. Anessa could take the route that went by Fred's Garage, where the cutest guys from their graduating class now worked. A casual mention of "pizza at the mansion" would pique their collective interest; perhaps even raise her social standing a notch or two. If she worked this right, a friendship with Jenna would bring her all of the attention she deserved.

CHAPTER 5

My Darling Wife and I

There was an understanding between people in Pepperville who saw each other every day. A wave or a nod, that was the acknowledgement of the intimacy that exists from occupying the same insignificant space in the world. But most often this didn't involve actual conversation.

We noticed when someone gained weight or hadn't gotten enough sleep. We knew each other's names and the color of each of our respective homes. We just didn't talk about it unless it came up in the process of pointed conversation.

"You know Jenna Thompson?"

Of course I did. Everyone did. This was standard coffee shop dialogue.

"Did you hear that she..."

Of course I heard. Everyone heard.

There was a rumor going around for a year, maybe two that Jenna wasn't allowed to attend school. The best gossip had it that she was confined to the mansion all but one hour a day, allowed out to see the sunshine just like the prisoners, at four p.m. sharp.

I knew that wasn't true because there were times when we would be scurrying to work and noticed a scrawny girl walking off the Ashton property. My wife always commented on her unusual gate and the look of death on her face. It was on one of these occasions we had our first face-to-face conversation.

She always walked at the same pace, not slow, not fast, her red backpack centered perfectly on her boney shoulders. There was something solitary and familiar about her gait, just as my wife suggested.

Jenna Thompson possessed the solemnity of a woman on the way to funeral, even though we knew for a fact that she was headed to the relatively upbeat world of Pepperville High School.

My wife always said we should invite Jenna to dinner. We never had any children of our own but often hosted nieces and nephews for the summer and frequently enjoyed the company of their vacation companions.

I guess My Darling felt sorry for Jenna, the hollow-eyed girl who lived in an empty mansion. I had never given it much thought. I wasn't one for idle conversation at that point in my life and didn't care to share a meal with someone who appeared so, well, for lack of a better term, odd.

Several times My Darling commented that she was sure the girl needed a friend, that we should stop and offer her a ride. I just shrugged my shoulders and kept on driving. It wasn't our place to find her a social life. We were unfamiliar with the world of high school what with its strict hierarchy and social standards.

Every day my wife waved at her, the way people do in small towns. Jenna never waved back, nor did she acknowledge our existence on the road beside her until the one exceptionally cold winter day when we were late pulling out of the driveway.

We weren't three blocks down the street when we spotted Jenna, evidently late as well, because she hadn't taken the time to button her wool coat and it flapped open and closed with each gust of wind.

"Pull over."

I never disagreed with My Darling, especially when she used her deep, authoritative voice. I didn't want the cereal-for-supper consequences that were sure to follow my disobedience.

I cranked my window down, breathing in the sharp, winter air. "Do you want a ride?"

She glared at us with mistrust. I couldn't say that I blamed her. I was wearing an old leather hat, the kind that had flaps covering the ears, and a red and green plaid winter jacket. My wife had buttoned her coat up to the top button, forcing her saggy chin to over-flow onto her beige coat. We almost perfectly matched in color and texture. Our old station wagon sputtered and whined in the bitter weather, and I'm sure we appeared like a circus act ready to take center stage.

"I...can walk."

I started to roll up the window, anxious to extricate myself from a seemingly innocent situation that had become uncomfortable.

My Darling leaned across me and put her hand on the window, now allowing it to move any further.

"Get in, honey. It's too cold to walk and I know for a fact that you're late." She used her low voice again.

Jenna stared at the ground, like she had been scolded and said nothing. But then she surprised me and reached for the door handle to the back seat of our green station wagon, a car we had purchased to transport various teens a lifetime ago.

She pulled her heavy backpack in after her and instantly the car filled with a sweet smell, a combination of maple syrup and hairspray. She didn't ask who we were; we didn't offer to tell.

"So...you're a senior?" My Darling asked.

"No," Jenna replied. And after an awkward silence, "I'm a freshman."

I glanced at her in my rear-view mirror, only able to view thick furrowed brows. Her voice was smaller and less mature than I had imagined. Her surly and yet somehow confident demeanor as she walked to school every morning belied a more commanding vocal presence.

"We have nieces and nephews staying with us during the summer. They come from all over the country. You'll have to come to dinner and meet them. I'm sure you'd enjoy hearing about their adventures."

My wife was masterful at this type of conversation, but on this occasion, her cheerful banter was met with stony silence.

"Aren't those Ashton boys good-looking? The few times I've encountered them, they've always seemed so intelligent."

Jenna sighed, obviously irritated. "They don't speak to me. I'm—we're just the help."

"Never? They've never talked to you? I can't believe they wouldn't..." the atmosphere in the station wagon suddenly seemed far too heavy for an early morning ride.

"Do you ever think about getting out?" I blurted out.

My wife stared at me in shock. She hadn't expected that I would attempt conversation as well. "Getting out of the house, I mean. Going somewhere with friends."

She shrugged. She began to tap her foot nervously against the back of my wife's seat.

Jenna seemed a different breed than the loud and lazy teens draped over my patio furniture every summer. I sensed she wanted to get out, get on, do something besides just exist. Or maybe it was the car and the old person smell she couldn't wait to extricate herself from. I wasn't sure what made her so unsettled, only that it intrigued me and I wanted to know more.

"Maybe there's somewhere else entirely you'd rather be." I continued.

"A girl your age should be enjoying parties and shopping."

We pulled up in front of the high school, and she opened the door before I had even taken the car out of gear. My wife opened her mouth to speak but stopped mid-thought when it appeared her captive audience was about to make a run for it.

Jenna got out quickly, slinging her backpack over one shoulder. She turned and hesitated a moment before shutting the door.

"Thanks," she said quietly.

I was surprised she didn't run at that moment to the front door of her high school. She was at least fifteen minutes late (according to my calculations) and had just endured a ride with an obscenely friendly older woman.

Instead, she leaned down so that her head was almost at eye level with my wife. She placed her hand, small and feminine looking, on the window that my wife always left cracked open regardless of the weather.

The shape of her face was identical to that of her mother's. Now that I was able to examine it up close, I could see that the two of them shared a remarkable resemblance, except for the eyes. Her mother's had been a sparkly deep blue and full of possibilities. Jenna's, though a beautiful brown, were hard and closed off like two exotic looking marbles; something to admire but completely cold and uninviting. Even this fact fascinated me. She was insecure and self-righteous at the same time.

"I do think about it," she said simply. She turned and shut the door with barely enough force, walking up the concrete stairs at the same pace she had walked every morning. I admired that part of her instantly. She wasn't going to let anyone tell her how fast life should unfold.

I imagined those Ashton boys didn't intimidate her one bit.

I was hoping this was all about my never having a child of my own. She was young and vibrant and beautiful, and at the same time sullen and repressed. I was hoping I needed to know more about her because she was mysterious. I couldn't think about it being anything else.

Later I would search the back seat for any clues this mysterious girl had left behind. There was nothing there but a few strands of hair, almost the same color as mine had been in my youth.

"What does she think about?" My Darling asked as we pulled away from the curb.

"Leaving," I replied. "Moving on."

"Oh."

We rode in silence until we reached her parking lot. "So she doesn't want to come for dinner?"

CHAPTER 6

Chief Blank

The police chief, who had a staff consisting of himself, his secretary, and her cat, Gendarme, was frequently seen drinking a warm Royal Crown Cola from a bottle that hung on a clip, attached to his belt loop. Being the police chief in such a sleepy town was not a difficult job, and would have been especially easy if he were patrolling in a city vehicle.

But Chief Sean Blank monitored the forty-seven named streets of Pepperville perched on his bicycle.

There was no money in the budget for a police cruiser; the last time it came up for a vote it was decided the money would be better spent on a seven-foot lighted Santa for the holiday season. That wasn't really a problem since Chief Blank didn't have a valid driver's license anyway.

He had grown fond of his blue three-speed. His well-tanned, muscular legs were displayed unabashedly from underneath official enforcement-blue, thigh-length shorts. The chief never varied his attire in colder weather, other than to add a matching dark blue winter jacket.

His feet were similarly clad in dark blue shoes, but they weren't police issue. These were biking shoes complete with a metal clip on the bottom, giving him the illusion of a serious bike rider. He learned the hard way that a foot pursuit was not possible while sporting this particular choice of footwear. On one occasion, the chunk of metal on the bottom of his right shoe caught on a sidewalk seam during a heated pursuit, sending him flying into the air and out on the street. He nearly missed becoming the second vehicular death in Pepperville.

During this episode, his old, ankle-length pants snagged on the manhole cover and he vowed never to subject himself to such a job hazard again. From then on he wore biking shorts every day, no matter what the weather.

If someone honked a car horn from right behind him, as anyone under fifty might be tempted to do, Chief Blank jumped in surprise, spilling warm soda down the front of his official police uniform. His complaints to his secretary were duly noted, though the raucous teens (as most all of the offending honkers were) rarely received punishment for their actions. Tickets were more likely to be issued to the offenders within his reach, like jay-walkers or someone trying to shoplift a carton of milk from the Shoppe and Walke.

"Dag-blastit! Can't a feller drink his soda?" he would complain, wiping the stain with his free hand. It happened so often the city added an extra forty dollars to the police budget the following year, for the purchase of two new police shirts.

Shortcomings aside, Sean Blank was a handsome man. Women, especially the elderly, made a point of going out of their way to ogle Chief Blank on his bicycle. He had—or rather, the city had—recently invested in expensive brown biking shoes with metal clips attached at the sole.

Even the men of Pepperville admired his chiseled physique, nodding their approval as Chief Blank rolled down the block. Police on the popular cop dramas of the day had big bellies and ate lots of bakery items. Not their patrolman.

The editor of *The Pepperville Daily Times,* Emily Wigworth, printed pictures of him frequently, on at least page six or seven. Some of the captions were repeated, like "Chief Blank Apprehends Fugitive," and when he was on foot, "Chief Blank Apprehends Fugitive Sans Bike." No one complained about the frequency of his appearances, nor had they minded the repeated captions. He was, after all, the only representation of law and order in their community, and his services required some debt of gratitude from the city at large.

Chief Blank was a serious person despite his cartoonish demeanor. He didn't possess a sense of humor; a trait his father said would serve him well in law enforcement. At the age of twenty-one, he left his hometown; a small place similar to Pepperville in size but with an easy-to-read dot on the road atlas. (Pepperville was missing from most maps.) He joined the law enforcement academy and jumped at the chance to serve the town of Pepperville the day after his graduation.

It was a daunting task to become the sole source of law and order for an entire community at that age, so he tried to err on the side of caution when making an arrest. It had been ten years now, and in his mind, he was the epitome of restraint and good judgment. His father would have been proud.

Here's where the story takes a Peppervillion twist: Chief Blank had never, ever taken a day off. Even on the days his secretary stayed home, usually Saturday and Sunday, he was out patrolling on his bike.

The other shared peculiarity was the ability to live by a schedule. Without the interference of extra staff, his day became a familiar routine of patrol, protein bar break, patrol, coffee and a last sweep of the main streets before heading home at exactly 5:15 p.m. every day. Saturdays and Sundays didn't include coffee, since finer establishments were closed on the weekends and he refused to drink the cheap, watered-down swill at the truck stop.

This left little time for socialization, which was done by design. You see, our seemingly fearless Chief Blank didn't take a day off because the one thing that frightened him was dating.

Being a man of his stature, it was better not to try than to fail publicly when it came to dating. It was always possible he could make last page news showing up at a restaurant with a woman, a thought that made him shudder. He didn't want to embarrass his family, though his father encouraged him to try new things, like dating, in his new surroundings.

Ironically, Sean Blank was a man who very much craved the companionship that marriage would provide. I know that because I was there, in Fenderson's Flowers, Flowers and Fudge when he admitted it.

"This ain't the kind with peanut butter?" Chief Blank held a chocolate square up to his mouth.

"No, sir. We use our homemade wine in that kind," Fenderson replied while wiping down a nearby table.

"S'good. I'll take another."

Fenderson glanced up, surprised to see Chief Blank finishing up the generous, one-pound portion he was served. Most newcomers to his shop were over-whelmed by the richness of his product and took most of their purchase home for another day, despite the quaint round tables provided for their enjoyment.

"That's your third piece, Officer. This stuff's full of sugar and good Iowa wine—you might want to take it easy if you've never tried it before."

"I want another one, sir," he insisted. "The plain kind this time." Chief Blank leaned back in his chair, cradling his blond head in his hands. "Don't s'pose there's a social outlet in this town."

Fenderson heaped the heavy chocolate square onto

a blue paper napkin and shook his head. "No, don't believe I've heard of one."

He nodded to me and I shrugged. I was far removed from that time in my life.

"My dad tell me that's where you get the experience. With women."

Fenderson raised one eyebrow. "What kind of experience would you be looking for?"

"Hand holdin'. Personal contact. That sort of thing."

Fenderson's face took on the blotchy color normally reserved for scolding his son. "Officer, I don't know what kind of candy shop you heard this was, but I never..."

And that's when Chief Blank, on an incredible sugar high, told Fenderson Reekblast the story of his fear of dating.

"I had a crush on a girl in my Earth Science class in high school. Lavernia Grunt. She had the pertiest blue eyes and when her braces came off, her smile lit up the entire lab."

He smiled, lost in his memories.

"I wanted to go to prom with her, but my mother said she was a farm girl who wanted to milk cows for the rest of her life. Mom wanted me to find someone who sewed and made cookies, that kind of thing." He finished his chocolate fudge and devoured the sample of Cashew Delite Fenderson generously included on his napkin.

"Thought it was my lucky day when we became lab

partners the month of prom. I had my speech all ready. 'Lavernia, nobody fills a beaker like you. Let's get dressed up and dance.'"

Fenderson bit his lip and if I wasn't mistaken, let out the tiniest laugh.

"Never did have the courage to ask her. We didn't talk at all, as a matter of fact. Turns out the two of us were equally shy. We didn't even finish our experiment because neither one of us opened our mouths. We gladly took an 'F' for the project, just to end the awkwardness. Boy howdy, was my folks mad."

It was the first time I'd ever heard of someone that frightened of the opposite sex. He was definitely working in the right town though. Every single one of us lived in fear of something.

CHAPTER 7

Donovan

Donovan's life had been mundane before the tragedy that sent him up our tree. After the wrestling meet, a late afternoon pizza party, and a jubilant trip home, life resumed its normal rhythm. The Bovants returned to work, ensuring the entire city—from garbage collectors to school board members to dentists—ran like clockwork. It wasn't until the following Saturday that things took a dramatic turn.

Someone heard it on the radio.

They told their neighbors, and then those neighbors ran out and bought a Stanswick newspaper. By 5:00 p.m., the news reached the Henry Bovant residence.

Saturday was Grandma Bovant's night to eat with Henry and his brood. Henry subscribed to all of the newspapers in a three-county area, so the conversation at his table was the most up-to-date of any of the Bovants who hosted Grandma.

"What's that, you say?" she asked, wiping meatloaf from the least of her chins.

"It's here in the paper. I'm outta breath. Just read it yourself," Trixie Phillips replied.

Grandma never liked Trixie's high-fallutin' ways and wasn't about to interrupt her favorite meal of the week entertaining her.

Donovan took the newspaper from Trixie's hands as she gazed at him with concern. "Thought you folks'd know already. What with your getting all the papers."

He hadn't even known the name of his State Wrestling Championship opponent until this moment. They mentioned it that day, but he never paid attention. It was just another one of his faceless conquests. His older brothers told him that was the best way to approach any sport; don't give them space in your head.

The second-place finisher ate pizza with his friends and left the gathering around midnight. He went home and kissed his mother and sister, telling them each that he loved them. Then he found an old tie he had given his father on his last birthday. He strung it around the beam in the attic. Sometime between 12:30 and 2:00 a.m., Patrick Dexter hanged himself.

Donovan's fingers shook as he read about Patrick's aunt, who was pregnant with her fifth child when she found her nephew's lifeless body the following day.

Patrick was prone to an endless cycle of depression,

the article continued, and his family had gotten to the point where they just left him alone, figuring he would come out of it sooner or later. The entire wrestling team gathered to grieve the loss of their friend.

The Stanswick state wrestling champion wept openly when he read further that Patrick's sister hid under her bed until the funeral was over. Donovan could take no more. He dropped the paper on the floor, giving it a sharp kick and turned abruptly to go upstairs to his bedroom.

"What's a matter?" asked his brother, Charlie.

Grandma Bovant got up and read over Donovan's shoulder, and now bent down to get the paper to finish the article.

"It's the boy your brother beat. Poor young man couldn't take the loss. The coaches put so much pressure on them nowadays." Grandma folded up the paper and headed back to the kitchen to continue her dinner.

Looking back, to most in his community it had been obvious that Donovan was suffering. He was never a cheerful person, but now he wore a constant scowl upon his face. His algebra teacher found herself avoiding his gaze; it made her feel cold and lonely. The high school girls who gushed in his presence dared not to approach him. He acted as though he could take their heads off in one fearsome bite.

Since it was such a large family, and since they were used to his odd behavior, none of the other Bovants gave it a second thought. They did stare a bit the first time they saw him after The Incident.

His coach mentioned that it was a "darn shame that boy up and hung himself." But that was all. In the Bovant family and the entire community of Stanswick, people just didn't talk about those kinds of things. The longer these ugly matters remained unspoken, the more likely they were just to go away. No one understood how Donovan had internalized this death. No one realized Poor Patrick's death was Donovan's fault for being so callous.

Unlike the rest of his family, he was bothered by a lack of connection with his opponents. After all, they were people too. Probably under just as much pressure as he was.

Donovan pinned this boy without a second thought, because that's what Bovants did. *Patrick Dexter.* Several times a day he repeated the name under his breath, trying to imagine what it would have been like to feel so defeated and deflated that you couldn't go on with life anymore.

As the days wore on, he became more and more reclusive. From the moment he opened his eyes in the morning he felt the weight of his culpability, understanding what others couldn't: he was responsible for this family's horrible loss. One evening, after doing his chores, Donovan sat down at the kitchen table. The rest of the family was watching football in the living room and nothing short of a nuclear explosion would startle them.

Bovants were known for their lack of attention to

the outside world not only during sporting events but also during regular television viewing. When they gathered around Uncle Marvin's big twenty-seven inch to watch the VHS tapes of Bob Hope's Christmas specials, not even the town's tornado siren could roust them.

Donovan carefully wrapped his wrestling medal in tissue paper and placed it in a balloon-covered HAPPY B-DAY! gift bag. He thought momentarily about adding a note but decided against it. The next morning, the gift bag sat on top of his dresser. His bed was neatly made and the dresser freshly dusted. One window was slightly cracked to let fresh air into the stuffy second-story room. The glass of water sitting on his desk had blown over sometime in the night, leaving a dark stain on the faux-wood finish and blurring the American History paper on the Civil War he completed two days earlier.

By the time his absence was discovered, he had been gone for hours. He left behind the comforting circle of his large family and the familiarity of the city where he was born. He had a destination in mind. The State Wrestling Champ was about to begin a new life in a town known for its eccentricity. Donovan Bovant was going to become it's oddest resident.

This is a good place to order more coffee and stretch my legs.

CHAPTER 8

Spiritual Bonus

I can hear the rush hour traffic and frantic pace of life in the real world. People are catching up from the weekend and I can hear lots of conversation. Some of it is interesting, some of it not fit for the ears of strangers.

It's good to be retired. It's also good to be able to watch life move on without me. Kind of a precursor to death, only with my lack of religious convictions, it's hard to say what my vantage point might be from the other side.

I never went to church regularly in Pepperville. Although one's absence was duly noted every Sunday, no one ever asked me why I wasn't there. Eight churches framed the perimeter of our small community. A preacher from one of them lived next door for many years, but when he died they couldn't find anyone to replace him. For some reason, coming to Pepperville was a demotion.

From what I hear, folks just took turns each week-end, preaching to each other, like an à la carte kind of service. The coveted black robe was passed from house to house until everyone who was anyone had worn it.

For those who attended, absence was excused on the days a special sports event took place. State wrestling was one of those times. My mother only cursed on those occasions.

"Damn churches closed their doors today. There'll be no cheese at the store for at least a week."

I grew up in a small, blue house across the alley from Ashton Mansion. It looked like something that at one time had been a proud addition to the Ashton property. But by the time I entered high school, the paint was peeling and the porch was a sad, sagging remnant of its former self.

My father announced he was replacing the rotting boards when I was seven. By my tenth year, he'd purchased the lumber. When I was in high school, my friends and I erected a "keep off the porch, unsafe" sign.

My mother often reminded me that my father hated the Ashtons and that, to him, the ragged porch was a symbol of his defiance of their wealth and pros-perity. When we finally had enough money for a tomb-stone for dad, I offered to frame it with the faded porch wood. My mother did not appreciate my sense of humor.

At that time, Jenna's mother was young and pretty; an "imported" servant from the Ashton's

Chicago house. Although she never publicly confirmed the story, rumor was her parents died in a freak accident. One of the Ashton mechanics (there were four on staff) had been fired for joyriding with Ashton automobiles on the weekends. He was the one who told this story while drowning his sorrows over a large pitcher of beer.

Jenna's grandparents were buffing out the remnants of Mrs. Ashton's futile efforts to learn to drive. It was an all-day task, one which they undertook every time Mrs. Ashton had several drinks and decided she'd drive around the block. Employees were instructed to keep the keys out of her hands, but she became enraged and none of them were brave enough to challenge her.

After an arduous morning, Jenna's grandparents were seated on the ground enjoying their lunch. One of the Ashton sons, home from boarding school, stormed out of the house and jumped into the vintage Cadillac, putting the car in reverse. The car crashed through the garage door and over the unsuspecting employees. Both were killed instantly, and Jenna's mother had no other surviving relatives.

Mrs. Ashton repeatedly reminded anyone who would listen (or so I've been told; I never actually met her) that "charity begins at home." By this, she meant any home where she wasn't residing.

She sent the young orphan to the Pepperville mansion to work as part of the staff. I don't think Jenna's mother, Vivienne, ever finished high school, because even though she was just a few years younger than I, never once did I see her carrying books down the hall.

I only spoke to her once. It was just after she moved to Pepperville. We both ended up carrying out our trash at the same time. My mother insisted I do my chores before meeting my friends, which felt like a personal attack on my social life.

We arrived at the communal dumpster simultaneously.

The irony wasn't lost on me: though she was carrying the refuse of a grand castle and mine came from a run-down hovel, we were both headed to the same place. The first thing I noticed was her large beautiful blue eyes. I'd never seen any quite that size, but my assumption was that everyone in Chicago possessed them.

Years later I would recognize the same message in the eyes of her daughter, the same hopelessness.

There was a scent in the air like my mother had when once a year she did the "deep" cleaning and brought out the expensive cleaning products. It was comforting for me because it meant we were having frozen dinners that night. The next best thing to eating at a restaurant in my day.

Both of us reached for the big dumpster lid at the same time.

"You go ahead," we said in unison. I laughed. She lifted the corners of her mouth, smiling ever so slightly. I could see the hint of two dimples, one on each side.

"Go. I'll wait," she said quietly.

"I haven't seen you around before," I replied awkwardly, knowing full well who she was. I lifted the dumpster lid as high as my arms would reach, so that she would remain in my view.

"No. I'm new," She turned her head away, either bored by our conversation or unwilling to continue talking to a stranger. Apparently, she had not yet discovered that I was irresistible; something the girls in my class had found abundantly obvious.

I gestured for her to empty her trash as I held the lid open for her. My mother would be impressed by my chivalry.

"We always meet at the bakery after school. Do you want to go sometime?"

"I can't."

She dumped her trash and pivoted back toward the giant fortress that acted as her prison. I noticed her hands were rough and an angry red. They reminded me of my mother's hands after a day of arduous laundry and housekeeping.

The lid dropped, me letting go without realizing it.

Not wanting our time together to end, I yelled, "You're pretty, Vivienne!"

She didn't respond, not even to ask why I knew her name.

I felt an unexplained sadness after our meeting. On a number of occasions, I offered to take out our garbage at exactly the same time that I'd met this intriguing girl. My mother had an inkling this was about a girl, but I was offering to do a chore and she wasn't about to rock the boat.

Fear of the Ashtons kept us kids from approaching the gate. Rumors swirled about the presence of security personnel, equipped with the latest in James Bond technology and shoot-to-kill orders from an unknown higher power. Of course, none of them were true.

Other than a padlock on the front gate, there was really nothing preventing anyone from making an unannounced call upon an Ashton resident. I certainly possessed the ability to scale the white- painted, metal fence.

But I was young and ignorant, so I fantasized about this mysterious girl for a few weeks and then completely forgot she existed. As with all unattainable beauties, we teenaged boys eventually turned our attention to someone less perfect who would actually return our affection. We needed physical contact.

It was three years later when I heard from the plumber that she was pregnant. "A secret boyfriend, sneaking in the back door at night," he said, as he tightened the washers on our new kitchen sink. I knew that wasn't true. She wasn't the type. There was more to this story, because the girl from the trash can didn't have the energy for late night meetings and certainly wouldn't have been interested in a nefarious backdoor lover.

It made for great bakery gossip though. And there were years of speculation over just who the mysterious father could be. I bragged that I'd met Vivienne before, that I knew her deepest secrets from our time together. At one point, my crude group of buddies and I took bets on which delivery man the child would resemble.

Wait, where was I? Oh, yes, church.

Vivienne didn't attend church either. Whether it was because she was a fan of local sports or because she didn't have a day off, I'll never know. What I do know is that Jenna had a secret she kept from Vivienne.

It was the Sunday of state football playoffs and I was on my way to buy canned cheese spread for my wife when I spotted her out of the corner of my eye. She was coming out of the back door of the Blinding Church of Light. Just a little snippet of a girl, she almost escaped without notice, but as she rounded the corner, a stern-looking woman grabbed her by the arm.

I had to intervene.

Pulling my car over to the nearest parking space, I walked over to the girl and recognized those same blue eyes. I smiled at her and just like her mother had done years earlier, she looked away quickly.

"What seems to be the problem, Mrs. Eddison?"

"This little girl stole from our cupboards. I was just tidying up since there's no service today and this little thing scurried in like a mouse." She walked two fingers across the space between us. "The girl's mother should know she's stealing."

Knowing she would shrink from my gaze, I looked away as I asked, "Did you take something you needed?"

Jenna opened her hand to reveal two, peach-colored ear plugs.

Curious, I asked, "Do you know what these are for?"

She nodded, though still gazing at the street. "To keep noises out."

Mrs. Eddison's interest piqued, she bent down by Jenna's side. "What noises, child? Is something terrible happening where you live?"

Jenna studied Mrs. Eddison's concerned face. "Football, wrestling and basketball. Mrs. Ashton screams at the television when she watches. Neither of us laughed at her demonstration. Somehow, we knew it would hurt her feelings.

We agreed she could keep the earplugs she'd found. I wondered to myself if Jenna also found the quiet of the church to her liking and maybe her childish curiosity got the better of her. According to Mrs. Eddison, there were placed in the pews for those who had a sensitivity to the choral performances.

One thing was for sure: Jenna hated wrestling.

The Television Event of the Year

According to my sources, Jenna only attended three wrestling matches in high school. The first one was during her freshman year. It was required for biology class that they take cotton swabs and swipe the wrestling mats for germs to look at under the microscope.

After the next week's Biology lab, she swore she would never attend another match, or touch the mats again for that matter. But it was only nine months later, during her sophomore year that she fell head over heels in like with a senior on the wrestling team. He was popular, outgoing, and extremely handsome. He was the kind of boy who didn't notice her kind of girl.

She watched him pin his opponent, fantasizing that he would nod to her after his win. She was seated two rows behind the team, after all. Jenna watched, at first with dismay, as his new girlfriend from the drill team came down to high-five him, and then with complete depression as he elbowed the young man seated next to him as he bragged about their exploits.

Once again, Jenna swore off wrestling. Her mother tried twice to get her to attend again, hoping that somehow Jenna's appearance in the muggy, sweat-reeking high school gym would gain her social acceptance.

Jenna refused until the last meet of her senior year. Her English Lit class won the Longfellow Young Poets award given by the state. It had only happened once before, when her mother was a mere twelve-year-old. This information did not induce Jenna's excitement, but the threat of failure in English Lit I for non-attendance did. The class was forced to sit in the gymnasium until the end of the 145-pound match, at which time their efforts and more importantly, those of their teacher were recognized.

The usual "gym smell of too many people without a good deodorant" hit Jenna's nose as soon as she opened the passenger door of her mother's car. As an honorary attendant, she was waved past the booster club mothers who were collecting tickets and cash, and Jenna grudgingly made her way to the gymnasium. She found the other lit class members seated three rows behind the wrestling team, looking just as enthusiastic as she felt. Anessa waved excitedly at Jenna from the student section. Jenna mustered only a flip of her wrist before looking down at the ground, where her gaze stayed for the next fifty-seven minutes.

When the class and their achievement was

announced, the teacher, energized by his moment in the spotlight, ran over to the announcer and whispered in his ear. To the horror of all seventeen members of English Lit I, the announcer was now calling them by name to the center of the wrestling mat, where the 145-pound match had just ended with not one but two, bloody noses.

The crowd applauded weakly when each name was announced. Jenna stepped over the rows of bleachers until she reached the floor. Preparing for her unwanted walk to the center of the gym, one of the wrestlers stuck out his spandex-covered calf. She tried to hop over it, but he lifted it in retraction at the same time, catching her in the most undignified of areas and sending her flying backward.

Whether it was intentional or just an unfortunate occurrence, the wrestler and his teammates began to laugh. Jenna slid up against the bleachers and her cheek caught a rather large sliver. When she came to a halt she froze for a moment, trying to absorb everything that had gone wrong within a short ten-minute time frame.

Her crotch area was throbbing, as was her forehead. As she tried to stand, she realized there was something resisting her return to the upright position. Her hair was caught under the bleachers and she would need assistance.

It wasn't until her struggles to sit up resulted in tiny squeaks of protest that anyone noticed. To the rest of the gym, she looked like an overly dramatic teen who wouldn't remove herself from the floor in an attempt to extend her moment in the limelight. She could hear the wrestling team laughing and the rest of the crowd whispering, she was sure, quite awful things.

After what seemed like an eternity, one of the referees returned from the locker room having disposed of his blood-covered uniform. He immediately recognized the problem and motioned for help. A man with three teenage daughters of his own, he could empathize with Jenna's situation and stayed with her until the principal arrived.

It turned out that the only way to extract Jenna from her worst nightmare was to cut off that portion of her hair. The bleachers could not be moved unless everyone was evacuated and it was already nine-fifty-five. Everyone just wanted to finish the meet and go home.

So the principal called the janitor, who unlocked the Home Ec room where a nice pair of sewing scissors were found. By this time quite a few people had gathered around, and the coach had given the wrestlers a stern warning about laughing at this poor girl. It just so happened that Eula Wilber from the Cut 'n' Shine beauty shop was seated in this section and came down to help. She offered to make the cut and also to trim up Jenna's hair the next day to match.

When Jenna was finally extricated, short-haired and lumpy-fore headed, the crowd applauded in sympathy. The red welt on her head was no match for the blush of embarrassment all over her cheeks. As she was walking from the gym down the long hallway to the nurse's office she heard an even louder roar when the wrestling meet was allowed to continue.

Her mother did not speak to her the rest of that evening but looked enormously guilty. She went out the next day after Jenna's trip to the beauty shop and bought her three new outfits and never mentioned public appearances again.

The three outfits still hung in the closet, barely worn. It was a bit of a shrine to her mother. Now, instead of fashion, her focus was orderliness.

Tuesdays were always cleaning day for Jenna. As she entered the back door of Ashton Mansion, she noticed the telltale droppings of a mouse on the kitchen floor. She was continually amazed at their persistence; after all, the kitchen had been relieved of anything resembling food long ago.

Jenna took her cleaning supplies from the closet and put headphones on. Calley graciously loaned her one of her motivational tapes, *Six Easy Steps to Unbelievable Happiness.* There were only a few more hours of natural sunlight in the house and four floors to clean so she would have to keep moving.

No need to pay for electricity when Jenna was the only human inside the premises. During the winter she would come two hours early, just to make sure she had enough daylight to complete her chores. When her mother was alive, the two of them could breeze through the work with daylight to spare. Her mother took pride in her work, and little else, it seemed.

Jenna understood her mother's passion. The smell of lemon and bleach cleansed her own soul as much as it purified the massive home. After stripping the bed sheets from all seven beds, she scrubbed the walls, the floors and occasionally the ceilings. The sheets would be washed on Fridays, during her weekly trip to the laundromat.

On chilly days, she chopped firewood to use in the grand, cherry-wood-and-marble fireplace. Eating her cold supper beside the fire was one of her favorite things to do. She usually ate pimento loaf and a banana, but sometimes she'd have some leftover she brought from the cottage. She always brought her own utensils and put them back inside the plastic container to wash the following morning when she went home.

Saturday was the one day when Jenna didn't have a set schedule. It was usually a day for catching up, reading, or visiting the Pepperville Public Library. This particular Saturday was different.

Jenna looked at her watch. It was already twelve-thirty and Anessa would be arriving soon. They made plans to meet at noon, but Anessa was never the punctual type. Jenna tried cutting the brownies she'd baked. Twelve pieces, exactly. They needed three more minutes in the oven, but Jenna was just as impatient to get her baking over with as she was the whole state wrestling experience.

She took the spatula and started scooping chunks onto the yellow-edged "company" plate she had retrieved from her mother's bedroom earlier in the day.

Her mother always stressed the importance of good company plates and silverware, but Jenna never had any company after her mother died so her hard-earned treasures had been gathering dust in what was now Jenna's spare room.

The doorbell rang at the same time the knob turned; like Anessa wasn't sure Jenna would open the door on her own. Jenna shook her head.

"It's me, Jenna. I brought pepperoni."

Jenna paused for a moment, depressed by the finality of a specific food about to enter her home. There was no getting out of this now.

"Coming," Jenna replied. She opened the door to find Anessa's edible contributions hanging from the doorknob in a quickly stretching plastic bag. Anessa was holding her enormous purse and two overstuffed, red pillows displaying "Mindenbury Wrestling" hand stitched in brown thread.

"Did you make those?" Jenna asked, half interested, half horrified.

"Of course not." Anessa pushed past Jenna flopping the pizza in the chair by the door. "My mother did. Two years ago when that really cute kid from Mindenbury won for the third time or somethin' like that. But anyway, he was good lookin' and Mom thought if she stitched pillows and sent them to the boy's mother, he might call me."

"Oh." They stood in silence for a moment. Jenna took the pizza and headed for the kitchen.

Anessa flopped down on the well-worn green

couch and turned on the television. Jenna returned with the company tray containing pop, pizza and her mound of brownies. Anessa eyed the pile of steaming brown with some reservation but said nothing.

The two girls loaded their plates as the smallest wrestlers began the event. "See? I told you this would be fun!" Anessa said enthusiastically between bites of pizza. Jenna reluctantly agreed. It was much better than sitting in her mother's old room, as she did many Saturdays.

They discussed what former classmates were doing, how each liked their job, and the strange customers Anessa had to deal with. An hour passed quickly, with only occasional glances at the television screen.

Anessa offered to get more drinks when she noticed that Donovan Bovant was up next to wrestle. "He's the one from that big family, you know? He has an older brother; gorgeous guy with red hair and muscles out to here." She raised her right hand several inches above her left shoulder to demonstrate "out to here." She flexed her thigh, muscular from so many hours of standing at the checkout counter, and pointed her toe like a bodybuilder. "Do you think mama would mind makin' me a redhead?" She tousled her bleached hair and several pieces fell to the floor.

Jenna let out a hearty laugh, surprising herself.

"He's too young for you," Jenna replied. "And besides, you don't want a muscle-head, anyway. Those athletes are so full of themselves."

"Well, he's hot. Mama says if you want to stay young, you need sassy perfume and a younger man." She shook her hair and sniffed first to the right and then the left, just to make sure the Love's Baby Soft she sprayed liberally earlier in the day had not worn off.

"And I want a good-lookin' man like him. I already have my weddin' dress, you know. I ordered it from the Penney's catalog with my graduation money. It's in one of those special plastic bags in my mom's closet."

Anessa had apparently abandoned her plans to get more soda. Jenna got off the couch and started to move toward the kitchen.

"Wait! Don't you want to watch him?" Anessa asked, alarmed that her friend would leave the room at such a crucial time.

"I'm getting something to drink."

Anessa shrugged. "Suit yourself, then."

Jenna stood in the kitchen for several minutes. She could hear Anessa whooping and hollering, carrying on a conversation with the television. It made her extremely uncomfortable. In the Ashton house, emotions of any kind had been discouraged. An outburst like Anessa's would have meant banishment from the main house until such time as the exuberance was under control.

"HE WON!" Anessa screamed.

Jenna rejoined her in the living room, carrying with her a look of disdain.

"He won!" Anessa repeated, shaking Jenna's shoulders. "That family is amazing! Can you imagine the kids we could have? Talk about your super-jocks. Our whole family would be hot. My mama would be sendin' pictures to every relative we have, just to make them jealous. Harley and Candy, that's what I'd name my little red-headed kids."

"Great," Jenna replied unenthusiastically, shoving residual brownie goo in her mouth and removing herself form Anessa's grasp.

"I'm goin' to call my mom. She needs to make another pillow," Anessa said. "Can I use your phone?"

Jenna nodded. She sat down on the couch and watched as a three-tiered podium was moved to the center of the ring, and the blond boy from Stanswick stepped on the top step. His eyes met the lens of the camera and Jenna felt a shiver go down her spine. They weren't especially notable eyes, run-of-the-mill blue, but there was an acute sadness in them. They seemed to push his lower eyelids closer to the floor; the chin strap, that now hung loose, looked like a lever that if pulled, would empty the contents of his entire washed out face onto the sweaty mats in front of him.

A State Wrestling official placed medals around the necks of the three boys standing at the podium. They announced his name, "Once again, Donovan Bovant!" and began playing the National Anthem. The crowd screamed and girls ran from the bleachers to embrace all three boys as the camera pulled back.

A sadness gripped Jenna and, once again, she remembered her experience in the gym: all eyes and sympathies upon her and yet she was alone in her humiliation. Why did that matter now? Why was this high school boy, an athlete with hundreds of cheering fans and a loyal home-viewing crowd, of any significance to her?

Anessa was chattering away on the phone. "I think we should make them just like the pants—with *wick* on the front and *Stans* on the back. Two with team colors... Uh huh. Should I send him a picture too?"

Jenna grabbed the remote control from Anessa's hand and turned off the television.

His sadness was obvious to her, but evidently not to the cheering crowd around him. Not to Anessa, chatting mindlessly on the phone.

Jenna stood. "I'm leaving. Going to the Shoppe and Walke." She needed air and a clear head. She stared hard at Anessa, hoping she would get the message that it was time to go. Anessa seemed oblivious and continued to chat with her mother, the woman she lived with and had seen two short hours before.

She grabbed her coat and walked out the door without looking back.

CHAPTER 10

The Day Everything Changed

Squish. Squish. Squish.

It was unusual that Jenna would run out of furniture polish; she was so careful about planning just the right day to purchase each item. There were still three rooms to finish and if she were to put them off until Wednesday, then Wednesday's schedule would be disrupted as well. It was unsettling that she could forget something so easily in such a tightly controlled environment.

The thirty-one brick buildings that lined Main Street, fifteen on one side and sixteen on the other, were a hodgepodge of one- and two-story businesses. Jenna had been only five when the sixteenth building on the north side of the street collapsed.

Greg Prembone, Anessa's brother had not understood the concept of the brake pedal during his driver's education course and subsequently plowed into the corner of the vacant two-story building. Jenna and her mother witnessed the entire event from across the street, and fortunately survived the experience unscathed.

Her red boots slapped the pavement as she walked down Main Street. The wind was more vicious than usual, causing her to wrap her wool jacket tighter around her deceptively frail body. She reached the Shoppe and Walke, a small one-story building in the middle of the center block of Main Street. A branch from the huge maple tree, the one sitting prominently in front of the old brick building completely blocking the *Shoppe and Walke Grocery* sign, slapped her in the face. The tree had outgrown its position on the edge of the sidewalk and its roots pushed stubbornly through the concrete slabs.

She pushed it away, annoyed that the grocery store owner hadn't trimmed his tree the previous spring. After all, it *was* a city ordinance, and those not in compliance were subject to a $56 fine. Jenna was startled by a cough. When she looked up to see where it might have come from, she was shocked to find that someone had constructed a wooden platform about halfway up.

What shocked her even more, though, was the human form resting on the platform. *Was she imagining that?*

She could see Anessa through the double glass doors, asking for a price check a package of toilet paper as if it were any other day. Sniffing the air, Jenna was comforted by the scent of popcorn and dog food, the two factories on the outskirts of town.

Today, Main Street had the same smell and feel as if it were yesterday. But it wasn't. Today someone new had arrived to claim space where there wasn't any.

She had seen homeless men on television before. *Did they move from town to town?* The interloper had a muscular build though, not like someone who had spent their adult life on the street. The long brown coat he wore reminded her of a movie star, and yet the shoulders it was hanging from were not those of a proud national talent.

The coat wore the man; bulky and ill-fitting. A hood swallowed his head, allowing a few wisps of blond hair to escape on either side. She took a tentative step closer and studied his profile. He had a long slender nose and thin, chapped lips. There was something familiar about this drifter; something she couldn't place.

She stood for a moment, scanning her memory for all the men in Pepperville. After a moment, his identity became clear. This was the wrestler, the one she had watched receiving his award only a few days ago. She remembered the sadness she felt watching him, though she couldn't put her finger on why.

What was he doing here? In a tree? In their tree?

She moved so that her body was in full view of him, staring hard. No matter how much anger she tried to convey in her hard stare, his eyes never met hers. Feeling complete exasperation, she whipped around and stomped inside the Shoppe and Walke.

Squishsquishsquish.

As she walked down Aisle 5: Cleaning Products and Toiletries, Jenna started wondering if this boy was participating in a television show, namely, "The Best Joke of the Season."

After an awkward show of affection or and exchange of words with an unsuspecting bystander, the host popped out from behind the tree declaring this "The Best Joke of the Season." There were usually celebrities featured, and maybe being State Wrestling Champ was a bigger deal than she realized.

When she reached the checkout, Anessa was on the phone with her mother. She motioned for Jenna to come through her checkout, though they never used the other cash register.

Anessa picked up Jenna's purchases one at a time. With the same hand, she typed the price into the cash register. Her other hand moved with animated gestures as she spoke. She squeezed the phone tightly between her head and shoulder, her appearance almost deformed.

"No, Mom, he was here when I got to work. I'm gonna take the pillows to him when I get off... 'm'kay. See you at five." She set the phone down to finish ringing up Jenna's items.

"My mom and I think he's out there because he got my letter. Donovan's waitin' for me to get off work.

Totally romantic, right? Fifteen-oh-six." She held her hand out expectantly.

Jenna peeked inside the brown paper bag. When had she picked up bread and macaroni? And imported tea? She was too embarrassed to ask Anessa to take the extra things off her order. This new presence was already a bad sign.

She dug into her pocket for the twenty dollar bill she had been saving for emergencies. There was nothing she could do, other than notifying Chief Blank when she left. It was really none of her concern. What did she know of athletes? Especially foreign athletes, from outside of Pepperville.

She handed her friend the money without looking up.

"What if he's not here to see you? He might be sick or confused..."

Anessa eyed her with suspicion. "Uh huh. I see what you're doing, Jenna Thompson. Well, don't you try to steal him, cause I saw him first!" She winked, easing the threat.

Jenna nodded, unwilling to remind Anessa that she'd never shown an interest in this boy in the first place. She walked toward the door, but then pivoted back. "Do you remember the story of Brad and Rosie?"

Anessa rolled her eyes. Everyone knew about Brad and Rosie. "They got in the back seat of the car together on a dare. Made out. Became hot-and-heavy boyfriend and girlfriend, perfect couple. Then she died a horribly tragic death, and blah blah blah. Pepperville's own tragic love story. Yawn."

It was expected that someday Rosie would announce she was pregnant and drop out of high school to marry her older boyfriend, who was already working in his father's plumbing business. Brad, for his part, tried hard to be faithful. But sometimes when he went on plumbing calls by himself, the older women proved too tempting. One of those women happened to be his next-door neighbor. Marsha was only too happy to report the affair to Rosie's mother after Brad tried to break it off.

The fight was vicious. Rosie took her pearl promise ring and threw it in Brad's face. He tried giving it back, but she refused to speak to him for several weeks. One day he decided to surprise Rosie with a rose and a new promise of fidelity. Instead of Rosie, he found Ruby, her older sister, who had been driving by her mother's home when she got a flat tire. After the tire was fixed, she decided to borrow a fresh blouse from her sister's closet, since they were both the same size.

Ruby answered the door and was overcome by years of pent up frustration toward her sister. She knew Brad was just a big dumb oaf, but a good-looking oaf. After a few minutes of half-hearted protest, he was easily overcome by her groping and words of encouragement. There was only one, heated encounter on Rosie's bed, after which they both felt relieved of their respective desires.

"Do you remember what happened with poor Rosie? After her sister got pregnant?" Jenna set her bag down on top of her red boots.

Anessa bent over and flipped her hair upside down to fluff it, before standing back up. "Not really."

"Her sister, Ruby married Brad and had three kids. He cheated constantly. Poor Rosie went to work at Pete's Diner and drowned her sorrows in lard. They even put it in the pancakes."

Jenna paused, expecting acknowledgment for offering this nugget of information. When there was none, she continued.

"When Rosie was twenty-two, she collapsed while serving Pete's Breakfast skillet to a trucker just passing through. The public statement said that she died of a heart attack, but everyone in Pepperville knew differently."

Anessa was now staring intently at Jenna. "Go on."

"After the initial shock had worn off, the gossipers at the coffee shop started suggesting murder. Brad had been sending Rosie letters, professing his love and desire to be with her even though he had married her sister. Whether Ruby found out or not, the letters stopped after six months. Rosie grieved her loss and in so doing, ate her way into a barrier between her and Brad. He was very picky about the way women looked."

"That's what my mom says all the time." Anessa nodded solemnly. "You have to keep yourself attractive, otherwise the only man willing to marry you will be someone like my brother, Greg." She leaned forward and whispered, "she never says that around him."

"The paper said Rosie died of a heart attack," Jenna continued, "but everyone in Pepperville knew the truth. Rosie died of a broken heart. And nobody in town trusted Brad after that, including Ruby. All because of some letters."

"So what does that have to do with me? And my future husband out there?" Anessa pointed out the window, in the general direction of the big tree.

"Your plan to write that stranger a letter, maybe? Love letters were the cause of Rosie's death and Brad's downfall. You don't want to get yourself in the middle of something."

When Anessa didn't seem convinced, Jenna added, "he could be a murderer for all you know. I'm convinced he'll be gone before morning."

Anessa raised her eyebrows. "You should be getting on home. Call me and we'll do something again soon, okay?" She turned to greet her next customer.

Jenna stormed out of the store.

She knew Anessa had been sending letters of adoration to the family, maybe even to Donovan himself. But the more she thought about it, the less she thought that Anessa's goofy letters had something to do with his situation. It had to be another girl, a relationship gone bad. She sensed tragedy and felt oddly connected with this stranger. But Jenna, normally a kind-hearted and sweet girl, felt no empathy. Instead, she was filled with rage.

Donovan claimed the biggest branches of the biggest tree on Main Street, without asking the the residents' permission. He'd most likely broken branches to get to his perch too. This Donovan person was a menace to their peaceful city.

How would she go to the store again, knowing he was up there, watching?

She paused underneath the tree. Her eyes traveled up quickly until they reached his perch. At some point, probably when unsuspecting Pepperville was asleep, he had nailed two boards into the tree as makeshift steps. He was sitting on three or four he had nailed together, as sort of a platform. Pretty energetic for a guy who was now sitting like a statue.

Jenna couldn't see his eyes, the eyes that drew her to him on television. He was focused on something across the street—a squirrel maybe? His hood covered most of his face anyway. Was he planning to say anything? Or just sit in their tree, in *her* tree, all day?

She looked at her watch and noticed it was ten-forty-five. The chief would be finishing his workout right about now. It would throw a wrench into her normal schedule, but she was duty-bound as a citizen of Pepperville.

Jenna turned left on Maplewood and walked half a block until she reached a two-story brick home. There was a sign on the rickety gate that read, "Weights out back." She took that to mean that the weight lifting equipment was literally sitting in the back yard. But when she reached the back yard, she was greeted by a large, unhappy Rottweiler and clotheslines criss-crossing the space.

Jenna noticed a side door that was propped open with a jug of maple syrup and an empty pop bottle, and the familiar blue-green, law enforcement three-speed leaned against the house. She knocked tentatively before entering.

The house had a split entrance; the steps going toward the basement offered the most promise, with clunking and grunting sounds emanating from that general direction. When she reached the bottom of the stairs, Chief Sean Blank and Fenderson Reekblast were heavily involved in some sort of weightlifting ritual, and neither of them had noticed her entrance.

Fenderson Reekblast was lying on a bench, and Chief Blank stood over him, encouraging him to push a bar with small weights on either end.

"You can do it, Fen, just a little farther!" Chief Blank said intently.

Fenderson grunted in the most undignified manner and let the bar come down to rest on his chest. "Nope. Not today."

Both men noticed Jenna at this point, and Chief Blank took a towel and began wiping his sweaty forearms after he called her over. "Needin' some instruction, young lady?" he asked.

"No!" Jenna replied, horrified that he would assume she wanted to join them. Then in a more composed voice, "Actually, I wanted to inform you of a violation."

"Oh?"

"Yes, sir. There is a man...well, he's more of a child really. He is sitting in the tree in front of the Shoppe and Walke. I thought that maybe...well he's breaking some sort of law, right?" Jenna looked at the floor. She could smell their strong man-sweat, a form of intimacy she did not wish to share with city officials.

Chief Blank lifted his shirt enough to reveal a rippled abdomen and wiped the sweat from this area also. Jenna looked away, wishing she had not chosen to inform him of Donovan's presence at this particular time.

"Jean, is it?"

"Jenna, sir."

"Far as I can see, that boy didn't violate no laws. We passed that ordinance a few years back making it legal to sit on public property. Mrs. Welbee wanted to eat her lunch on the Thomas Jefferson statue every day. Now that don't mean you can pee on public property though. Does it, Fen?" he turned to his friend, who was still trying to catch his breath.

"You're never going to let me forget that, are you Sean? My boy lost his car for two weeks after that stunt." He replied grumpily.

"I didn't see him actually climb up the tree. Now *that* would be a crime." Chief Blank smiled. He had very straight, white teeth.

"But I—"

"Can't do nothin' unless I see him committin' the crime. He's probably just pullin' a high school prank.

We ignore 'im, and in a day or two he'll be out of our hair."

Jenna paused. She remembered the hollow look in Donovan's eyes when she first saw him on television, the pure sadness and desperation. If he were still in the same condition, it was unlikely he possessed the mental energy to get down on his own. But that surely wouldn't prevent someone else from doing it for him.

"You didn't see him climbin', or doin' anything else he shouldn't?"

"No, sir. I just noticed him this morning."

"Thanks for comin' by then." Chief Blank smiled. He was obviously more interested in continuing his workout than arresting a criminal.

Jenna did not reply. She was infuriated that he had brushed her off so easily, and bothered by the fact that she was so affected by his sweaty body.

As she left the brick house she kicked the pop bottle out of the way and let the screen door slam behind her, causing an immediate reaction from the back yard dog.

Still needing to vent her frustrations, she continued her rampage by shoving the city-owned three speed to the ground, slightly bending one of its spokes. Although there was no indication either of the gym's occupants had heard her, Jenna panicked and rushed out the gate.

Jenna Thompson was now part of the criminal element of Pepperville, which, before today included one shoplifter, two unlicensed dogs and a mail thief.

All the way back to the mansion this weighed so heavily on her mind that she didn't realize she had left her purchases, including her furniture polish sitting next to Chief Blank's bicycle. Her heart raced as she thought of spending the night in jail, or worse yet, being paraded in handcuffs down Main Street while Donovan watched from his perch.

Already his presence, Donovan's presence, had caused irreparable damage. She had been forced to meet the police chief in an entirely too intimate setting. Now he would never take her seriously. And she had damaged city property, something the "old" Jenna from yesterday would never have done. Jenna surprised herself by letting out a big sob, followed by several more. Her shoulders heaved. Her nose ran. It took at least twenty minutes to regain her composure, and then she began to think carefully about her predicament. She was not one to lose control. Maybe she would turn herself in to avoid the embarrassment of arrest.

There was the more pressing matter of getting this boy, no, this interloper out of the tree. What if he became violent?

He was a danger to the unsuspecting community. Her whole life of living underneath the radar had lead up to this moment. It was up to her and her alone to make sure he left.

Anessa was already acting differently, the Chief was neglecting his duties, and then what would happen if he became violent? Someone planted in a tree like that could lose their temper on a whim and hurt a passerby, and what perversion was happening on that branch? And then there were environmental issues of his living conditions...

The job of removing him would have to fall into her unseasoned hands. She could see that now. She realized that for the first time in her life she was more than capable of completing a task.

CHAPTER 11

Anessa

Anessa took the time to apply an extra coat of Azure Blue eye shadow before leaving the break room of the Shoppe and Walke. She rubbed an index finger across her yellowed teeth, disgusted by the stains.

The last magazine article she read while waiting for a customer said swallowing toothpaste made your teeth white from the inside out. From her locker, she removed a tube of Aquafresh toothpaste and squirted a liberal amount into her mouth. Although she had been informed of the risks of eating toothpaste, she swallowed it all in one large gulp after the appropriate swishing time.

"You have to make sacrifices for beauty, Anessa," her mother always reminded her.

The Kleenex (four on each side) she had placed in her bra at the beginning of her shift were flat and sweaty so she took this opportunity to restuff and re-plump, molding each cup carefully until it each side was uniform. One more quick hair check, and she was ready to clock out.

The pillows her mother meticulously stitched remained at her check stand, and she picked them up after a brief reminder to her replacement checker that coupons from last Saturday's *Pepperville Daily Times* were no longer valid.

Anessa walked outside across the street and positioned herself on the curb in front of the store. It was the perfect spot to view him.

Something about his long, brown coat reminded her of a John Wayne Western that she had seen on cable recently. There were chills going up and down her spine.

She pictured herself walking into Pete's Diner with the tall, good-looking outsider holding her hand. People would whisper and stare at the new face as they always did. Then they would realize that he was one of the famous wrestling Bovants. They would wonder how she, Anessa Prembone, caught such a fine specimen of manhood.

"Hi, Donovan," she said in her softest, most breathless pitch. There was no response.

"Hi—it's me, Anessa Prembone," she said again, a little louder. "You probably remember my name from the letter I sent. Did you get it?"

She became aware of the bangs hanging in her face and she shook her head to adjust them. "Of course you did," she continued. "I sent it right after state wrestling." She cleared her throat, as her mother had recently reminded her of the allure of a clear and feminine-sounding voice.

Donovan didn't move, nor did he acknowledge her words. She was beginning to wonder if he had a hearing problem. The announcers never mentioned it during state wrestling meet, but she had missed the precious minutes of his pre-match introduction when she was in the bathroom.

"Well, if you're deaf, I'll just write notes and send them up, kinda like the family that lived in the tree. What were their names? I think there was a Bobby... That's okay though, I don't mind. We know all about different in my family. Wait 'till you meet my brother, Greg."

She decided it didn't matter if he looked at her. Maybe he was the shy type, and those boys always warmed up after a few minutes of conversation.

"You have five kids in your family, right? You're second to the last. Everybody has red hair except you. I think blond hair is better anyway." She giggled, fingering a strand of her own questionably blonde locks.

"I've met your grandma, ya know. She comes here to shop all the time. Or at least she used to. Haven't seen her since you..." she paused. "She always talks about you. 'My boy Donovan this' and 'you should see how strong he is now.' My grandma never talks about me like that. Me and Greg are her only grandchildren, and she acts like we don't exist most of the time."

Anessa cleared her throat once more.

"My mom says Grandma didn't want kids and then didn't want grandkids, so that's why she never comes for Thanksgiving or Christmas. You're so lucky to have that big family."

Anessa glanced at her watch. It was almost six and her stomach was growling. There was leftover pot roast at home, and she wanted to find it before Greg did. At this moment, her appetite took precedence over her future husband.

"I'm leavin' these pillows with my phone number on the front. When you come down, call me, 'kay?" She took two steps back in order to enjoy one more gaze admiringly at his physique. At this point she realized that he was sound asleep, his arms tucked under his armpits and head resting against a branch. His long, blond eyelashes rested against his cheek just like the cherubic angel paintings in her grandmother's living room.

Anessa was nothing if not stubborn. Especially with a prize like Donovan at the end of the branch. She felt if she were persistent, as her mother always lectured she should be, he would come to his senses and realize the bounty standing before him. Anessa Jones was a the full package: a hard worker who didn't give up easily, good "birthing hips," whatever that meant but her great aunt always mentioned them, and an undying devotion to her intended.

On Anessa's end of things, there were no other potential mates on the horizon and she didn't want to let a catch of this magnitude pass her by. When Donovant Bovant—THE Donovan Bovant—showed up on her doorstep with flowers and candy and a great big smile, the entire single-female population of Pepperville would sigh with envy.

Every evening as she left work, she dropped a note underneath the tree. Sometimes she just told him about some practical joke her miserable brother Greg had perpetrated on her. Other days she professed her undying love and her willingness to wait for him, no matter how many weeks it took.

Since the pink stationery coated in Love's Babysoft always disappeared by the time she showed up for her shift the next morning, she knew they'd been read. She imagined his amusement at her jokes and the smile that crept over his beautiful face.

It had to be the highlight of his evening since he didn't seem to communicate with anyone. She imagined his wooden platform covered in her musings so he could read them whenever he felt alone. Donovan's longing for her was only surpassed by her devotion to him; the silent misunderstood tree dweller and the woman who waited patiently for him to descend into her arms.

CHAPTER 12

Calley

alley set the mats out, fourteen for today's class. She knew that Flora Wilson had the stomach flu and Anessa was a wildcard, so she stacked an extra mat against one of the long, studio mirrors just in case. She paused to admire her figure: tight breasts, minute stomach lump, and incredibly muscular arms. What a beautiful woman she was for fifty.

Her husband often commented on his good fortune; finding someone like her before the rest of the world figured out that she was something special. They met in the seventh grade and married in April of their senior year. Calley couldn't wait any longer to leave the rigid environment her mother had created; she wanted to start her own business as her worldly, slightly older cousins in Stanswick had done.

She devoured all of the magazines and videos they sent her, those that didn't sell in their sporting goods store. By the time Calley was twenty, she was ready to open her own studio. She had all sorts of ideas for classes and wasn't upset when the first class, *Calleyrobics,* attracted only two attendees. She still paid the motel for the use of their conference room. There was never a single day when she was down or depressed; that wasn't Calley's style.

Over the years, her exuberance for exercise, and life in general, helped her to build a successful business. She was always eager to learn something new and even more excited about sharing it with her clients and friends. She felt the instructional videos and magazines she read were purely a suggestion.

A person of her advanced position in the world of exercise could certainly add her own unique twist to each new technique. Her husband, while never once making an appearance at *Calley Sthenics,* was nonetheless quite supportive on the home front, insisting she preview all of her classes for him.

As she reviewed her new cooldown moves from the video *Breathin' Thru the '80s,* she was surprised to see a crestfallen Anessa walking through the door. Normally they shared an exuberance for life that Calley admired.

"Hey, girl. You're in my class early for once. Gotta date later?" Calley asked with a wink.

"Who would want to date me?" Anessa replied, her voice breaking.

Calley took her arm and guided her to the broom closet. "Tell Miss Calley what's goin' on," Calley said soothingly. She noticed out of the corner of her eye that Jenna had walked through the door, and she motioned for her to join them in the closet.

Anessa was always one pinhole away from a dam burst. Calley happened to be the pin that day. She cried as she explained to Calley that there had been many long letters and now a new bottle of perfume, and still no attempt on Donovan's part to cement his relationship with her.

"Y'all need to remember to breathe deep, like we do in class, and look him in the eye," Calley explained. (*Strengthen Your Relationship and Your Abs, 1984*) "He's been readin' your notes, that's somethin'!" she said encouragingly.

"Calley, I'm not even certain he has eyes. Maybe the birds pecked 'em out. He won't look down long enough for me to see." Anessa looked down at the black-and-white-checkered tiles, moving one foot in a circle.

"Maybe I don't know how to...how to talk to boys. Maybe Greg didn't know what he was talkin' about when he said..."

Calley noticed out of the corner of her eye that Jenna was shifting from one foot to the other. She was about to erupt, something that had been happening with more frequency. As Jenna's self-appointed mother figure, Calley was beginning to feel some concern.

"What was that, girl?" She asked Anessa, which resulted in the same confession. This time, neither of them realized Jenna's presence behind them.

"You're being ridiculous! We have to get him out of the tree and out of Pepperville, and you aren't helping!" Jenna snapped.

Calley and Anessa whipped their heads around and Calley cursed herself. She'd allowed herself to be distracted and now the volcano was erupting,

"This fool thinks he's a bird, or a twig, or whatever and the more attention you pay him, the longer he'll stay!" Jenna growled. The dark circles under her eyes made her appear menacing in Calley's fluorescent lights.

"Now, honey, let's don't make Anessa feel worse," Calley cautioned.

"Why can't anyone else see how offensive it is to have a stranger living here? Like that? Things have a certain way they're supposed to work in Pepperville. The town functions because we all belong, like pieces to a puzzle. We're all meant to be here doing what we're doing. He can't just show up whenever he feels like it. That's not the order of things here."

Jenna pivoted toward Anessa and stuck a dainty finger in her chest. "And you—why can't you hunt for a man elsewhere? Preferably at ground level! This is all your fault!" She turned and stormed out of the studio, pausing only long enough to restack her mat before kicking the door open.

Anessa's jaw dropped, but she remained uncharacteristically silent.

Calley's considerable experience included dealing

with crises of this magnitude. There was always at least one lady in class with man troubles.

"I don't know what's got into her. She's needin' some serious yoga, I think." Calley shook her head. "You can just go ahead and like whoever you want, girl. They can live in a tree, on top of a car, or wherever!" She patted Anessa on the back.

"He does like me," Anessa insisted. "He reads my notes and one of the other checkers told me that when I'm on break, he climbs down to a lower branch, like he's wonderin' where I went. He does." Anessa sniffed. "Just because he won't look at me doesn't mean he doesn't like me."

"You don't even need to worry about looking at his eyes. I'm sure he knows you're there." Calley cleared her throat and pulled her shoulders back. "Any hay— keep your options open! There's more than one fish in the tree, if ya know what I mean." She winked knowingly at Anessa.

Calley flashed back to Anessa's high school years, when it was widely gossiped that the girl was juggling five football players at once.

"Thank you, Calley. For everything." She wiped her eyes, smearing black eye liner all over the napkin. She glanced over Calley's shoulder. "I know it's not FFAF day, but a girl has to keep up her strength...

CHAPTER 13

Jenna

Not only was it insulting that the police chief wouldn't take her seriously, but also that this Donovan person must know he was committing a crime. He was a constant thorn in her side; a bad dream that wouldn't go away. How was it that the rest of the town seemed to function normally, despite his presence?

No one had ever been homeless in Pepperville. At least not as long as anyone could recall. There was always a relative or friend willing to take in the down-on-their-luck folks.

The closest case was Roger Stuntworth, who lived in his car temporarily; two days to be exact. Rumor had it that Roger got drunk after hearing of the death of Eugenia Rupert (there was an entire bar full of drunk people, all claiming personal involvement with Eugenia) and bragged that he was going to make a memorial to the girl, in his own backyard. His original idea was to build a memorial of stones and concrete blocks, but at 2:00 a.m. the probability of locating these supplies was next to nothing. Roger's next idea was something big and flashy, something involving fireworks.

When he couldn't find any in mid-September that would shoot off sparks, he decided to create his own. First he piled the decorative rocks from his garden (six in all, counting the two he stole from his neighbor's back yard last summer) into a heart shape. Then, he took a bottle of his best Aqua Velva aftershave, stuffed a rag in it and placed it in the middle of the heart. After mumbling his own eulogy to the little girl he had seen twice at the library, he lit his creation and waited for heat and emotion to overtake him.

Anybody who has lived in Pepperville for over a month knows that the wind kicks up after midnight. Even Roger, in his drunken stupor, had to realize that the hairs on his head were not flying around because he was moving rapidly.

A good gust caught the bottle and whipped it up in the air. It sailed over and landed on Roger's blue jeans, the ones he had removed for comfort purposes during the altar construction, and started them on fire. (Those who go to church say it was the spirit of Eugenia. I just like to think of it as life kicking him right where he deserved.)

Roger was slow on a sober day. For some reason, he thought that he should take his pants into the kitchen sink and douse them with water. By the time he reached his kitchen, his arm was engulfed in flames and he dropped the pants on his grandmother's best doily tablecloth.

When he sobered up he was too embarrassed to ask for help, at least for those first two days. After trying to nurse his injuries from the back seat of his station wagon, he finally asked for assistance from his neighbor, the one he stole the garden stones from in the first place.

The reason I tell you this story is because Jenna found herself strangely drawn to Eugenia Rupert as well. Not only could she sympathize with the girl being terribly unlucky in life, but she had been just as unfortunate in her death. Poor Eugenia had the distinction of being the only person buried in the Pepperville cemetery without the privilege of a real casket.

The night before Eugenia's funeral, the Stanswick senior class snuck into Pepperville and removed all three of the caskets from Ed's Funeral Parlor. The next morning, the three caskets, much the worse for wear, sat on the lawns of each of the three senior class teachers.

Eugenia's family insisted that she be buried, casket or not. And since nothing like this had ever happened in Pepperville before, no one disagreed. So Eugenia was wrapped in her mother's beautiful star-patterned, hand-stitched, Spirit of '76 yellow-gold quilt and buried in the Pepperville cemetery.

The fact that she had no casket elevated her status in Pepperville; she was communing with the earth in a way no other body in the cemetery had. The last page of the paper read, "Local Girl Resting Peacefully. Casket's Whereabouts Still Unknown."

It was some time before there was sufficient communication between the two towns and the exact nature of the prank was discovered. The caskets were returned and the scratches buffed out. The seniors were forced write an apology to be placed on page two of the *Pepperville Daily Times*, and to pick up trash along the highway leading into Pepperville; a grand total of three pop cans and an old baseball mitt. Initially there were angry words on the streets of Pepperville, but eventually, the emotion died down. The general consensus was that kids from all towns have been known to do stupid things in the name of a senior prank.

This requires a certain delicacy, so I'll try to tell you in the most respectful way. When Chief Blank refused to help her and the rest of the town seemed to be wearing blinders, Jenna decided to take matters into her own hands.

She had to leave evidence that Donovan was desecrating public property. At first, she thought about leaving...droppings around the tree.

Human droppings, to be exact. When she couldn't bring herself to collect them, the story of Roger Stuntworth's devotion to Eugenia Rupert (the poor dead girl) came to mind.

What if Eugenia, through the actions of Jenna Thompson, was able to rid the town of Donovan permanently? Jenna (and secretly Eugenia) could eliminate him and at the same time establish her (or their) legacy as the great protector(s) of Pepperville.

Being the resourceful girl she was, she devised a plan so outrageous it would have to get the attention of Chief Blank because of its audacity. No fireworks or a funeral pyre, but an attention grabber to be sure.

I can't honestly say I understand how she got to this point. She was such a good girl, always following the rules. But sometime in the week previous to her crime, she visited the cemetery carrying blue daisies from the Ashton garden. It wasn't hard to find the grave; it was covered with bouquets and teddy bears.

The following week at 1:55 a.m., she filled her shovel with the first bit of rich, brown Pepperville earth. She retrieved the few bones she needed, taking care not to be greedy.

It seemed appropriate to bring her mother's best apron, carefully wrapping the bones and placing them in her backpack. She patted them gently. It also felt appropriate to say some words of appreciation.

"Eugenia...Miss Rupert...This is Jenna...Thompson." She cleared her throat. "I want to thank you for your contribution to this worthy cause. I know you would want to help in any way you could; that is, to get everything back to normal. If we had done a better job of keeping strangers out, you wouldn't be in this predicament. I'm giving you back your power." Jenna turned to pick up her shovel again, and then added,

"And tell my mother I'm working hard, trying to make her proud."

She took pains to make sure the grave was covered correctly, each tribute in the same spot it had been before her arrival. On top, she placed her own arrangement and stood for a moment to admire her work.

It would be enough to prove Donovan's nefarious after-hour activities. Just who these delicate bones belonged to would be of no consequence; Chief Blank hadn't solved a serious crime yet. The suggestion of murder would be enough to send Donovan to jail or have him banished permanently.

This small offering seemed unceremonious. She needed a presentation so obvious, so awful as to cause the entire population to pause and ask themselves why they had allowed his dark presence for so long. She would start with trash from all over town and build to the discovery of the murder victim.

In the dumpster next to Pete's Diner, half-eaten hamburgers and empty ketchup packets filled greasy paper bags. Behind the fudge shop, she retrieved moldy candy and empty liquor bottles. Calley's trash contained pill bottles, once filled with the latest supplements. It was amazing what could be found after dark if one were curious enough. Ironically, the entire town would be represented as Jenna singularly ousted Donovan.

She plotted and planned, drawing out on paper the exact location to leave which item and on what night. Each identifying label or marking removed so that only she would know its rightful former owner. It would be gradual because one giant presentation would be too obvious. Donovan slept soundly above her head, oblivious to the military precision used to execute the plot for his demise.

After a week of product placement, she created the pièce de résistance with Greg Prembone's empty chew cans, labels removed, sitting beside the small tokens from Eugenia Rupert. It was an altar, a tribute to both Eugenia's continuing presence in the community and Jenna's ingenuity. She was oddly proud of her creation and was tempted to tell someone, or at the very least, take a picture. Instead, she walked back to the cottage in her red boots, unable to sleep the rest of the night.

Squish. Squish. Squish.

She showered, dressed, and sat patiently waiting for the morning light to expose Donovan for what he really was.

By 8:00 a.m. Jenna was out the door, walking confidently toward Main Street. There might have been the hint of a smile on her face. She went into the police department and inquired as to the location of Chief Blank.

"He's at the Shoppe and Walke, honey," his secretary said, not bothering to look up from her typewriter.

She decided to wait for ten—no, twenty—minutes, and then casually walk down Main Street to witness the arrest of Donovan Bovant for the desecration of public property.

She sat on the steps of the police station petting Gendarme and casually glancing at her watch. When she felt an appropriate amount of time had passed, she strolled purposefully toward the store.

What she found was a nightmarish scene.

The ground in front of the Shoppe and Walke, to her horror, was pristine. Donovan remained unconscious; she might go so far as to note he was sleeping peacefully. The law enforcement bicycle leaned up against the tree (still scratched) and all of her hard work, in more ways than one, had disappeared.

Jenna glanced pleadingly in the store and noticed Chief Blank filling his basket with fruit and Royal Crown Cola. She admired his new uniform, pulling tightly across his chest.

He held bananas above his head, scrutinizing their every flaw as if it were any other day. She fumed as she watched him survey the canned vegetables and pizza sauce. He didn't seem in any hurry to leave or arrest to anyone.

The shoppers going in and out of the grocery store likewise didn't notice Jenna any more than they would have on any given day. That's the problem with trying to melt into the background: when you want to get the attention of someone—anyone—it's like the lamp in the living room calling out for help. It's just another piece of scenery.

Her attempt at stranger extraction had failed so spectacularly. She had committed her second crime in under two weeks, and still, nothing had changed. Jenna was at a loss.

She entered the Shoppe and Walke and picked up a shopping basket. She approached Chief Sean Blank so quietly that he didn't notice her at first.

"Excuse me, sir?"

"Mmhm..." he was comparing canned spinach labels and didn't seem a bit concerned about the major development in front of the store.

"Uh, Chief...I was wondering. I was out walking this morning and noticed all sorts of—trash—and maybe other things under that tree." Jenna picked up a can of peas and put it in her basket temporarily.

"Well, Jean is it? I can see why that'd be upsettin'. Someone leaving a real mess of trash."

Jenna blushed. "No, I think there was more there than trash. I think that maybe Donovan is, well, doing bad things."

"Oh? Like what?"

"Like...um....oh there were cans there, of tobacco. He's probably smoking something toxic."

"I ain't seen no evidence of that." He moved to the next aisle, adding canned peaches to his basket.

"Yes, I think so. And he might possibly have...killed someone."

Chief Blank stopped and turned around. "What?"

Something had finally gotten his attention.

"Now, that ain't likely. The boy barely has the energy to breathe."

"No, I saw it with my own eyes. A bone lying there just this morning," Jenna insisted.

Chief Blank smiled. His smile was model perfect, just like the men who modeled sweaters in the Sears catalog. "Oh, that. I saw that too."

He patted Jenna's shoulder and it took all of her self-control not to shrink away.

"Just some chicken bones. Somebody's been eatin' at Pete's and leavin' their trash. Saw that a few nights ago. Got 'r cleaned up this mornin' already, so there's nothin' to worry about."

Jenna was burning inside. *Stupid! How could this happen?* This wasn't the way she had seen things unfold on the pages of the books she found in the Ashton library.

It was generally quite easy to frame someone for murder without going to the lengths that she had gone, and usually, the mastermind was happily vacationing in Europe or Eastern Pennsylvania before anyone figured it out. Her infatuation with the Police Chief ended that very moment. She turned and stormed off, slamming her basket on the checkout counter. This was the worst humiliation she had ever suffered.

It had been a month now since Donovan invaded Pepperville. Jenna fantasized daily about ways to remove him from his perch. She had gone to extreme measures, even going so far as to "borrow" from Eugenia Rupert. Although he never spoke and was little more than an amusement to most of the community, she wanted him gone. He was a thorn, a discomfort she couldn't shake.

There was no time for depression; fortunately, she had come up with another plan a block and a half from her house. She was drafting a letter when someone knocked on her door.

Anessa hadn't visited her in weeks and there wasn't anyone else who came to visit. At first, she thought about ignoring the knock, but the visitor was so persistent that after several minutes, her curiosity got the better of her.

She opened the door to find a well-dressed man exuding an intense woodsy smell that she assumed was expensive cologne. He wore a long, camel-colored coat that looked as if it had been crafted especially for him. His eyes were a light blue and his hair was side-parted, slightly graying at the temples. Her mother would define him as "a man who wants you to know he matters."

He carried a leather briefcase that matched the rusty brown color of his shoes. Even his hand, now extended in greeting, bore the polished look of a man of refinement.

"Miss Thompson?" The stranger asked in a strong, deep voice.

"Yes?"

"Warren Johnson." He shook her hand and she marveled at the smoothness of his skin. "May I come in?"

Jenna stepped aside and watched as he strolled

through her doorway with a confidence she had never witnessed before.

"I represent the Ashton estate. I'm sure you know that the Ashton boys have no interest in maintaining this property."

"Yes." Jenna suddenly felt hot.

"Drake Ashton has authorized me to initiate a real estate transaction with you, Miss Thompson." He set the briefcase on the back of her couch and opened it, revealing a mountain of legal documents.

"No, I–"

"The Ashton boys want to be rid of this place. The taxes are horrendous and they would rather sell than burden their heirs with its upkeep. I'm sure you understand." He smiled. A row of large, straight teeth gleamed. "They want to make a deal with you."

"This isn't my house. I don't want it." Jenna felt as though she was being smothered.

Tears burned her eyes "My mother and I—all we've done is keep it clean." *How much could one person take in a day?*

Jenna was reminded of the stuffy and pretentious nature of the huge home; uncomfortable yet familiar. Each room had been uniquely furnished, something like the Ashton version of the White House. Mrs. Ashton had taken great pride in the fact that she searched from one end of the globe to the other until she found furnishings that even to the most critical eye, looked identical in color.

The Aqua Room contained a large overly ornate

dresser, a queen-sized bed with a canopy, and two plump, velvet-covered chairs. Everything in the room was exactly the same color and shared the dated, paisley design. A source of pride to her was the fact that Teddy Roosevelt himself had stayed in just this room. His nausea and discomfort the next day had been attributed to the monochromatic scheme surrounding him that could, "drive the sanest of men to melancholy." Mrs. Ashton knew his over consumption of fine sherry the night before had been the cause of his illness and took satisfaction in the fact that he had taken notice of her exquisite taste in furnishings.

The Maroon Room was the master bedroom, and Jenna took extra care to make sure that the yak-skin rugs were safely rolled up and out of the way before she began the task of bleaching and scrubbing. The skins had been sent to India to undergo a unique dying process. Mr. Ashton was at first skeptical that the wild game expeditions he had participated in as a child should bear the mark of his color-coded wife. He had to admit that after some time he did find himself admiring their reddish/purplish tint.

"Yes, I understand. Things would stay the way they are until your twenty-first birthday. At that time, you would have to find yourself some outside employment to pay a very nominal mortgage payment. But the property will be yours. Permanently." He grinned and waited for her reply.

When none came, he continued, "The price they're asking is ridiculous, not much more than the price of a vehicle for the whole thing, all of the land is included. You have to understand what an opportunity they are offering you. You will own one of the finest properties in this entire county, if not the state of Iowa. We will finance your purchase so you won't have to go through the application process. No better deal to be had." He shifted his gaze around her living room. "Opportunities for someone like you...your age...don't come along every day."

"I'm not interested. Thank you." Jenna set her jaw and crossed her arms. "I don't want to do this." *It's too much. It's all too much.*

"I understand this is overwhelming. I'll leave the paperwork with you. We can talk again." The lawyer now spoke in a calm voice as if he had dealt with unreasonable women before.

"You're too young to appreciate this opportunity now. But believe me, most people in your situation would kill for the opportunity to own their own home. It's not often the maid gets to own the mansion." He set the papers on her couch and closed his briefcase. "I have some business to attend to in Stanswick. I only stopped here first to allow you to get some legal counsel. I can stop back in a few days," he said.

"I'm not going to change my mind," she replied quietly. And then, the timely nature of his visit struck her. "Sir, did you say you would be driving through Stanswick?" Jenna quickly finished her letter, composing two instead of the original three paragraphs she had originally planned. She gave it to Warren Johnson with strict instructions.

When he left, she hugged her arms around her body and stood with her back against the door. This new predicament sat on her chest like a lead weight, threatening to cut off all of the air.

She wasn't sure she understood why all of this was so upsetting. As a child, Jenna occasionally dreamt of her own place. Now she would own the mansion. The *owner*. There would be electricity, and life, and people knocking on the door. Asking for her. She would change the bedding on the enormous beds because she, Jenna Thompson, had slept in them.

Where her mother cleaned toilets and dusted lamps, she could lounge and eat potato chips.

She started to feel hot again. Smothered, actually. Jenna tore off her blue sweater, pulled down her knee-length gray wool skirt and threw them on the floor. Her breathing came quicker, harder, faster. She ran to the back door, where her red rubber boots stood and put them on, barely pausing to push her feet all the way to the bottom.

As she opened the back door, a sharp cold breeze met her unseasoned skin, but she didn't resist. She ran up the hill dressed only in her sensible undergarments and red boots. She ran to Ashton Mansion and into the back door. There was a small room off the kitchen where she and her mother would stay when someone in the Ashton family was ill and needed round-the-clock care. This room still contained a bed, a dresser, and a full closet.

Jenna threw open the closet doors and in a sweeping motion, took all of the maid's uniforms into her arms and pulled them toward her. Holding them tightly, she fell to the bed and began to weep. There were still strands of her mother's short gray hair on some of the uniforms and Jenna nuzzled these, trying to drink in her comforting scent .

What was the sound of her mother's voice? Was it a high, lyrical pitch as she wanted to remember, or was it the low no-nonsense sound of the woman in command of the Ashton staff? It had been too long. Jenna had been alone for two years now, with no one to remind her of her mother's funny sayings, or how she lightly rubbed Jenna's back after a hard day at school until she fell asleep.

This wasn't the way it was supposed to be for a nineteen-year-old girl. She should be preparing for midterm exams at a college with pristine lawns and imposing red brick buildings, or picking out a wedding dress with her mother and all of her closest cousins, giggling and whispering about her upcoming wedding night. Why hadn't this woman, who took such care to polish the massive chandeliers, given her only child something to hold on to?

Jenna's entire life was contained within these walls; memories and heartache and it began to squeeze from her the remainder of her persona.

Ashton Mansion was suffocating her.

Through her tears, Jenna tried to think of something positive that had happened here. Something to force her to sign the papers. Only one snapshot entered her mind—that of her eighth birthday party.

How many kids had been there?

There was a pink cake with animal cookie decorations. Mrs. Ashton had allowed the use of the formal dining room, provided Jenna and her mother were prepared to put in extra time polishing the silver after the party.

They were in the middle of Pin-the-Tail-on-the-Donkey when Mrs. Ashton stumbled down the stairs, her normally perfect mound of silver hair now squished flat against the left side of her head. There were drops of vomit interspersed with the blue, yellow and red polka dots on her polyester blend shirt. Her bright yellow pants were noticeably askew at the waist, and the blouse was only tucked into them on the left side.

She was completely drunk.

Jenna's mother offered to sit with her in her bedroom until the party was over. "All of these children will make you nervous."

"No, darling. I'm interested in observing. I've never witnessed a party for a bastard child." She smiled, revealing a slight gap between her two front teeth.

Jenna was used to her histrionics and hoped the old woman didn't notice the caramel-colored skin of her favorite schoolyard playmate. She was young and maybe just the maid's daughter, but already wise to the ways of her mother's keeper.

Mrs. Ashton perched herself precariously on a stool close to the children, laughing loudly as they missed the tail end of the home-drawn donkey. Her hands danced wildly in the air each time, as if she were performing in the high school musical. She grabbed one unsuspecting boy by the collar and jerked him to her breast.

"You have a nice little caboose. Probably very smooth." As she tried to reach down the back of his shorts, Jenna's mother pulled Mrs. Ashton to her feet abruptly, causing the little boy to fall to the ground.

"I'll help you take a bath, ma'am. Then we can do your hair," she said calmly.

"I don't want to go to bed. I want to converse with the chilllldren..." Mrs. Ashton protested.

"There are new bath beads," she insisted, lightly rubbing the old woman's back to appease her. When Mrs. Ashton didn't reply, Jenna's mother wrapped the old woman's arm around her shoulder and guided her away from the group.

All of the children watched solemnly as the two women climbed the massive staircase, the older spidery human leaning heavily against the body of the younger tired looking woman. They climbed slowly, one marble stair at a time. Mrs. Ashton's blue heels that she bought in Paris made a click-click sound as she raised each foot to the next level.

Jenna led her classmates into the kitchen, where

she sliced her own birthday cake. The children all ate in silence, shocked by what had occurred. The fact that they had tangible evidence of the great Mrs. Ashton's erratic behavior titillated the group, and soon the cake was forgotten as they were running and playing as care-free children should. All but Jenna, who was left to eliminate any evidence her birthday or her party existed.

While her friends played chase and pulled each other's hair, she fantasized about how different life must be outside of the mansion: Mothers fixing favorite foods and then waiting patiently in bed while the fortunate child picked out a favorite story.

Tonight Jenna would be helping her mother in the master bedroom after what was certain to be another monumental disaster. Any number of things would be tossed carelessly or even destroyed during Mrs. Ashton's drunken rants. More than likely, her mother would be needed the entire night just in case the old woman rose and didn't know where she was. Jenna would go to bed alone, as she often did.

After ushering all of the guests to the door, Jenna took the oversized butcher knife, covered in pink frosting and multi-colored confetti and washed it. She could not reach the dish soap so she cleaned it as best she could on her party dress before putting it back in the drawer. Jenna went to the closet and retrieved her mop and bucket and a dust rag. She dragged the huge kitchen trash can to the formal dining room and began to clean.

When she finished thirty minutes later, her apple blossom dress, size six, was smudged with frosting and wrinkled. She had wrapped her hair in rag curls the night before so they would make perfect tube-like swirls beside her face, just like those on Shirley Temple from the late night movies. Jenna imagined her mother taking pictures of her beautiful daughter after the party, as they sat together and admired her birthday gifts. Now her hair hung limply, weighted down from too much hairspray and perspiration.

She reluctantly climbed the stairs and entered Mrs. Ashton's bedroom, where her mother sat next to the bed, holding the old woman's hand.

"Did you have a nice time?" her mother whispered, using her free hand to pat the back of Jenna's dress absentmindedly.

"Mmhm," Jenna replied. They would all tease her tomorrow. It didn't matter though, she would sit alone at lunch the way she always did.

Her mother clucked her tongue in disapproval when she noticed the dress. "You'll have to wash this tonight."

"Such a good girl." Mrs. Ashton muttered.

"Yes, she is a good girl." Jenna's mother replied, squeezing Jenna's back.

"No one cleans woodwork like Jean." Mrs. Ashton slurred. She still hadn't opened her eyes.

"A...good servant...like your mother."

Jenna felt sick, dirty. She glanced at her mother and hated her for the smile on her face, her standard crinkled eye, no-teeth smile. It was the same smile she used when the dry cleaner delivered twelve pantsuits of varying color. The same expression her mother used when she said, "Thank you, have a nice day."

Why didn't her mother say something more? Tell the old woman how smart and pretty her little girl was? How much more she was than a vessel to hold the dusting rag? Instead, the two women shared an understanding, that this little girl was not so much a girl at all but a machine created strictly for the purpose of scrubbing and polishing.

There were no good memories at all. There was just pain.

A wave of nausea swept over her, and before she could make it to the bathroom, she vomited all over the floor. She hadn't done that since the day her mother died. Her head rested on the toilet seat as she tried to remember the feel of her mother's cool hand against her sticky forehead.

CHAPTER 14

Death

Soon after the death of Jenna's mother, I experienced my first nightmare. I had no right to dream something so intimate, considering she and I knew so little of each other. But the experience scared me. Haunted me really.

I saw Jenna lying in a field filled with fragrant red and deep purple flowers. Her tousled brown hair was flayed around her head. All four of her appendages reached out, touching the colorful carpet of nature. Jenna was squeezing the petals with her toes and fingers as if trying to extract another sensory experience from the velvety plants.

An uncharacteristically pleasant expression lit up her flushed face, and there was no denying it when the corners of her full mouth upturned. It was a legitimate smile. She was experiencing unbridled joy.

My unconscious mind struggled with the scene: why did she captivate me? Was this my brain's way of assuaging my own guilt over my behavior? Over events of which I had no control? Or was this purely a way to legitimize my uncultivated paternal instincts?

There was barely time to decide before the flowers began to extricate themselves from the field. Each one danced briefly in the air before finding a spot on top of Jenna, covering her up until only her eyes were visible. The scene played out in fast forward, taking only seconds to change from pleasant to gruesome.

Jenna was fighting to breathe, inhaling petals that covered her face until she made such an awful choking sound that I could stand it no longer. Her eyes begged me to help, and I could see the pain not only of her imminent demise but also of her short life wasted.

I turned and ran as fast as my legs would carry me, and though I could feel her staring at me, I didn't return to save her. I reached a wall of at least seven feet and fought to climb it, but my hands, small and delicate for a man, were unable to grasp the worn bricks. I couldn't leave this horrible scene but neither did I return to rescue poor Jenna. There I stood, screaming, for what seemed like an eternity. The only way out was to rouse myself from this state and that process became excruciatingly long.

I didn't sleep in my bed for a good month because this scene disturbed me so deeply. I was afraid to confront whatever this was. Falling asleep in the living room recliner became my nightly ritual.

Now that I think about it, that was a stressful period in my life. I was learning to live alone for the first time. I didn't know how to get out of bed without conversation, or in what position the toilet seat should sit. I understood how disconnected this young girl must feel from life and nothing more.

For the first time, I drove to the highway. I pulled off the side of the road and watched the cars passing by, a total of twenty-seven in one hour. They didn't slow at the sight of a middle-aged man in a station wagon, sometimes teary-eyed, sometimes half asleep.

The faces fascinated me somehow. Some were long, some were rounded. There were young parents grimacing while small were children bouncing in the back seat. Occasionally they were driving alone and wore an expression of complete concentration.

None of them were familiar. There was comfort in finding faces that hadn't been in attendance when Charlotte O'Cann sang *Oh Comfort Me* from under a darkened canopy at My Darling Wife's funeral. None of these travelers knew I had left my job on a Thursday afternoon and not returned in the month since. I was safely anonymous.

Eventually, the pain of my wife's death eased. The highway and its unfamiliar travelers held less allure, and I slowly rejoined the rest of Pepperville in performing mundane daily tasks. I nodded to Fend-erson and shook the hand of Chief Blank when he offered condolences. The only person I couldn't bring myself to address was Jenna Thompson.

CHAPTER 15

Anessa

The Shoppe and Walke was busy. Saturdays generally brought out the working folk, but today seemed to include the stay-at-home mothers and grandmothers as well. Anessa was flustered. Usually, by 2:00 p.m., she had read the *Tiger Beat* magazine from start to finish, and today she hadn't even glanced at the cover. By 2:30, she had completely missed her lunch break, and the loud growls of her stomach were starting to draw stares from the customers.

At 2:45, she leaned against her cash register to give her swollen ankles a break. Soon she would head to the break room with a can of Spaghetti-Os, whether the manager liked it or not.

"Excuse me, ma'am."

"Chief Blank!" She was surprised he was speaking to her; generally he paid for his items without conversation. "Do you need a price on somethin'?"

"Anessa, I think?" He was flustered. "No, no price. I've got somethin' else to talk to you about."

"Oh, god. Ohgodohgod. I seen this kinda stuff on TV. The policeman only comes to work to talk to you when somebody died. Who was it? Grandma? Greg? Please don't tell me it's Mama."

Anessa dropped to her knees and began to wail. Her low blood sugar combined with a flair for the dramatic made for a loud and raucous performance. Everyone in the store paused to see what was going to happen next.

"No! It ain't that. Get up. Please get up, ma'am!" Chief Blank hurried around the counter and lifted her up. His muscular arms flexed and several women stared admiringly.

He offered her his monogrammed handkerchief. Anessa shook her head no, and reached into her bra to retrieve her own supply.

"Just tell me. Tell me and get it over with!" she wailed.

"You're makin' this way too hard," Sean Blank replied. He ran his fingers through his thick, feathered hair. This scene had gone much smoother in his head.

"I'm on my lunch break, not on official business. I didn't even work out today. Because...because I came to see if you wanted to watch a movie with me...at the movie house...if you have the time, that is."

The sobbing and sniffling immediately ceased. Anessa had never considered him fair game because he was at least ten years older than she was, and he was a professional, way out of her league.

For the first time, she observed him as more than the local law enforcement. He was a man; one with well-defined biceps and a rear end hardened from years of serious bicycling. Why hadn't she noticed sooner?

"What?"

"I wondered if you would—"

"I heard you. I kinda have a boyfriend but..." Anessa immediately regretted saying that out loud. It was just that he caught her off guard, and she had always been taught to play a little hard to get once she knew she was going to reel one in.

"Oh, I didn't know that. Well, shoot. I'm sorry."

"No—I mean I did have a boyfriend—but he's busy, or—ohgodohgodohgod. What time will you pick me up? How do you spell your name 'cause Mama will want to make a pillow."

The first date ended on Anessa's couch in her living room, surrounded by surplus pillows Anessa's mother had sewn for "practice."

Some had misspelled names; others contained the wrong school colors. Beside the couple sat stacks of movies her mother deemed appropriate first date material, an odd combination that included *Fiddler on the Roof* and *Deliverance.*

"You're beautiful. Prettier'n any girl I knew in high school." He brushed her bangs from her eyes.

"Thanks. You aren't so bad yourself." Anessa blushed and rested her head on his shoulder. "I seen magazines before, with beautiful men. But until I seen—"

"Awww...that's crazy talk."

"No, let me finish. Until I saw Donovan, the boy in the tree, I'd never seen nobody that beautiful."

He looked taken aback for a moment, but quickly regained his composure. "He's a good boy, I think. Just confused. I've been tryin' to help him all I can. He sure leaves a mess every mornin'."

Sean Blank removed his arm from around Anessa's shoulder. She immediately pulled it back around her.

"There's more to this story," she continued. "He was the most beautiful man I'd ever seen, with long eyelashes and beautiful cheekbones. But that was before I knew I had options." She smiled and patted his chest.

"I look at those cans of creamed corn in aisle seven every day. That's my favorite, you know."

Sean Blank rubbed his hand up and down her shoulder and nodded.

"I can almost taste it with chopped up hotdogs and a bit of cheese the way Mama makes it." She took her fingers and lightly brushed his leg. The scent of Aqua Velva was becoming both overpowering and intoxicating.

"Then one day, a can of green beans drops off the shelf," she continued. "For the first time, I think about how good they smell when they're cookin', with bacon and onion. The creamed corn is still nice, but there are other things to eat in the world. I'm seein' things in a whole new light. That's what I wanted you to know."

The formerly lonely police chief squeezed her shoulder. "I can't think of anything nicer than green beans."

He never worked another Sunday.

CHAPTER 16

Marcus And The Boys

F red Baily, John Moran, and Luke Wright picked up Marcus Bovant early in the evening. As usual, there was no need to explain planned activities; they were athletes and, as such, afforded the luxury of unrestricted free time.

Stanswick High was legendary for its all-nighters, and luckily the drinking that ensued had never resulted in a serious car accident. Most students walked, since they were never more than a few blocks from home anyway. The vehicles were more for cruising, making out, and road trips.

On that evening, however, the boys had more sinister ideas. After downing a case of Miller beer for courage, they planned to find Donovan and bring him home. It wasn't like he wouldn't come home on his own eventually, but they knew it was the right thing to do, to preserve the dignity of the Stanswick wrestling team.

Donovan Bovant carried on his back the reputation of all Stanswick High athletics, and the identity of the entire town was wrapped up in the seasons of the football, wrestling, basketball, and baseball teams. Wherever he was, and they had good reason to believe he was in Pepperville, the entire town of Stanswick was represented on his letter jacket.

Luke's Aunt Deidre had taken his little cousin Shorty to the bathroom in the Quik Buy when she overheard the lady in the next stall telling her child that they would not be returning to Pepperville until the disturbed man was removed from the tree. The woman went on to explain to her daughter that she would not be allowed to live in their own backyard tree, nor would she even be able to take snacks up in said tree for entertainment. There was no telling why people went crazy, especially as young and good-looking as this boy was. It was sure nice of the Pepperville folks, she continued, to take care of him.

Well, Aunt Deirdre went home and told Luke's dad, who told Donovan's dad, who told Grandma Bovant. Grandma generally put out an all-points bulletin for big news like this. But running off the way Donovan had done was just plain cowardly. So, after she told three daughters-in-law and her next-door neighbor, the news died down and it was never spoken of in family circles again.

The group of rebel rousers had limited experience with "crazy" before. The lady with too many cats who lived next to the library usually kept to herself. And anyone else with problems was more about rumor than actual fact. If Donovan had indeed gone stark raving mad, they wanted to see it for themselves. Images of a young, bug-eyed man uttering incomprehensible phrases would keep the school abuzz for most the school year.

The group also pictured themselves as superheroes, who were about to rescue a fallen hero from himself. It would be easy enough to get him down from the tree, and John brought electrical tape to keep him confined. *But what would they do with him after they got him home?*

His family didn't want him back. At least his mom and dad didn't. Marcus had a tool shed behind his house he could probably use for at least a week. That was why his buddies included him. (Not to mention his ability to sneak beer from his dad's outdoor cooler.)

The trip to Pepperville was jovial. At speeds of sometimes seventy miles per hour, they reached the edge of town without losing their buzz. Marcus insisted they stop to relieve themselves on the side of the road. He sat down for a moment afterward and then laid down wanting to rest just a few minutes in the tall weeds. He was warm and groggy; a few minutes of shut-eye wouldn't hurt anyone. After several minutes of silence, there was a loud, familiar backfire. Marcus sat up slowly and realized his buddies, in the ultimate act of friendship, thought it would be funny to leave him there.

"Hey!" he yelled. "Dumbshits!" He heard beer cans

hitting the highway and saw them rolling towards him. But there was no sign of the truck that abandoned him. After several minutes, he realized the yellow pickup would not be making a return trip.

He rose unsteadily, and walked the rest of the way into town. When he reached the city after what could have been an hour or a few minutes, the streets were empty like it was a holiday in Stanswick.

All he wanted to do was sit on the curb and wait for his head to stop spinning. But the rumors about this town and the unbalanced weirdos who lived here were persistent enough to be true, so he knew he had to keep walking until he found a familiar face.

It felt like he was walking against a strong wind, he had to lean forward to stay upright. He could see Main Street and still no human forms to be found.

A fierce gust pushed tumbleweeds, rocks, and scraps of paper down the street hurriedly, like they had somewhere better to be. Every few minutes a howling sound emanated from in between the buildings, not that someone this inebriated would care.

When he could take the spinning no longer, he flopped down on the curb. The moment he sat down, all nine beers came back to haunt him at once. Somehow, he missed his clothes and his new brown "shit kicker" boots. After the vomiting mercifully ended, he was exhausted and wanted to lie down. He thought for a moment how funny it was (Irony would have struck someone with a higher level of maturity, but at seventeen, everything was funny.) that he was here to save his down-and-out cousin but ended up puking in the streets of a strange town.

He sat with his head in his hands, praying to the God he had previously only talked to on Sundays under protest, that this would be the end to his misery. He needed to deal with Donovan, and after that, how the two of them would get home.

"Do you need some help?" Jenna asked.

Marcus couldn't look up, that would have required super-human strength even a Bovant of his athletic prowess couldn't muster. Instead, he stared curiously at the feet in front of him. They were housed in red, rubber boots.

"I can help you find your friends."

He glanced up, immediately sorry he had done so because of the sharp pain that struck across his head like a bolt of lightning. "Ow...man..." He covered his face with his hands. When it finally passed, he was able to assess the face that accompanied the voice.

The girl had brown hair, beautiful brown eyes and an interesting face like he had never seen before. It could have had something to do with the copious amount of alcohol he had consumed, or maybe it was just a matter of him being grateful to lay eyes on another human being. One who was, hopefully, sober.

"Any other day I'd be asking for your phone number. How do you know my friends?"

"I just saw a bunch of idiots driving around yelling and making a scene. You kind of look like you belong with them."

This put Marcus in a difficult spot. He truly needed her help. But he was not accustomed to begging for it from girls with attitude. There weren't many of them in Stanswick, at least none he had encountered at parties or the ones who giggled next to his locker. He chose to ignore her comments.

"Yeah. My buds. Where did you see them?"

"I saw them two blocks that way. To the left. One was in the same condition you are, so I doubt they'll be going anywhere anytime soon."

"Thanks."

"Uh huh." She started to walk away, her boots squishing with each step.

"Oh—hey, miss?" Marcus tried to stand but thought better of it.

"Yes?"

"I'm looking for someone. He's kind of...crazy. Like nuts in the head. About my size, same big nose, and blond..."

Jenna glanced at him cautiously. In the waning light of the evening, his bright red hair shone brilliantly; healthier looking than the rest of him. His face had the same peculiar, angular shape to it as the wrestler in the tree.

"Hey, it's all right. I can find him myself. Thanks anyway." The more he looked at her, the more she intrigued him. She gave off dual messages: "I'm available," and, "leave before I shoot you."

"He's on Main Street, or rather, above it. You just need to walk one block over and three blocks up."

"Thanks." Marcus ran his fingers through his hair, conscious of her scrutiny.

Jenna stood with her hand on one hip, feeling awkward. She had so little experience with boys—*with men*— that she didn't know how to continue this conversation. and being laughed at by Chief Blank and his secretary was all the humiliation she could take for one day. But she couldn't stop herself.

"I could...walk you there." As soon as the words came out of her mouth, she regretted them. What was she thinking? He could be an ax murderer, or worse yet: someone who would pass an alley, shove her in, and "take liberties" as her mother used to say.

"Yeah. That would be great." Marcus replied. He rose slowly and turned to follow her. Now he noticed a brown stain on the front of his letter jacket. He'd have to get that dry cleaned before Grandma Bovant saw it, or she'd make his life miserable for ruining the expensive Christmas gift she'd given him.

Unconcerned about a drunken teen, Jenna pivoted and began walking at a vigorous pace. Both the abruptness of her departure and the speed with which she moved caught Marcus by surprise. He had to jog to catch up, an activity his stomach wasn't ready for.

"Hold up. Just for a sec." He bent over and put his hands on his knees.

"I don't have long," Jenna replied tersely. She had all the time in the world; just not for him.

"Okay." *You're a Bovant. Suck it up and keep moving.*

"So, do you go to high school here?" he asked. He tried to match her pace but fell several steps behind. She didn't reply but kept moving briskly in her red, rubber boots.

Squish, Squish, Squish.

"There. He's up in the tree." She pointed to a large tree in the center of Main Street, where an odd silhouette perched on one of the middle branches. This large bird or small human was hugging his knees and his long brown coat draped down onto the next branch. He had a hood over his head, and all that was visible was his sun-burnt Bovant nose. From a distance, it would have been easy to mistake Donovan for a vulture.

Marcus would have found this entire situation hilarious, if it had been someone else. Someone who wasn't a Bovant. He'd never dealt with someone in this predicament before, let alone the family star.

While he was trying to figure out how to approach his cousin, he heard the squeak of her boots again. She was leaning forward, willing her body to move faster as she stomped down the block.

Yeah, that it. This weird chick was stomping instead of walking. In rainboots that weren't even needed in this part of Iowa.

"Hey—would you want to go out sometime? Like on a date?" he yelled after her. "My name is Marcus!"

"No," she replied firmly, without looking back.

The rest of the family will love this story. Pepperville is everything Grandma said it was.

He pictured the family gathered around the table for dinner and how he would entertain them, perhaps embellishing his experience. Then he remembered that his cousin was sitting in a tree in this crazy town.

"Donovan!" he called up. There was no response. "Hey, bud! It's me, Marcus! We were on the football team together last year. Your dad and my dad..." he stopped.

How out of it was this poor guy? Should he talk to him like his five-year-old sister?

"You gotta come home. Nobody friggin' lives in a tree." There was still no response. Marcus sat down. Removing someone from a crisis situation looked so much easier on TV. "You're killin' me, man!"

After a few minutes of silence, he heard the rusty muffler of the yellow truck and saw his friends driving down the street. They didn't look as cocky as they had when they dumped him outside of town.

Luke got out of the truck first. "What the hell...?"

"You shitheads left me!" Marcus yelled, trying to divert their attention from the tree. "Someone couldn't knocked me out and thrown me in the cellar!"

"Man, what's up with your cousin?" Fred pointed to Donovan. "How we gonna get him down?"

Marcus thought for a moment. "I'm gonna climb up there and talk to him."

The other boys nodded, confident that Marcus could "talk him down" like the firefighters did on television.

Marcus easily scaled the branches with no signs of

his earlier stomach upset. When he reached his cousin, he maneuvered his body into the sitting position beside him on a small, wooden platform.

"Remember when Grandma Bovant built us that treehouse? You were six, I think." Marcus smiled as the memories came back.

"You told everybody you weren't going up there, no way, no how. Then your little sister climbed up and we all laughed at you. The next time we went over to play and there you were. Your mom couldn't even bribe you with orange popsicles to get you to come down."

Marcus realized after he'd told this story that perhaps it wasn't the best one for this particular situation. He glanced over at his cousin, whose features appeared frozen. He wasn't even sure Donovan had blinked since he arrived.

"Just come home with me, bud. Do you know your dad has already cleaned out your room? You better come home before he rents it out or something."

He knew that in reality, no one spoke of Donovan. This wasn't how a Bovant behaved, so they pretended like he wasn't a Bovant at all.

Marcus searched his mind for something that would hold meaning to Donovan. He thought of family functions, girlfriends, and all of the normal high school activities. None of them had ever held any appeal for Donovan.

"Do you remember my sister, Sadie? The snot nose

with them braids on the side of her head? She asks me all the time—where'd my cousin go?"

Marcus continued, even though the reaction he had hoped for was not forthcoming. "Yeah, she cries sometimes at night. Why is my cousin crazy? Why doesn't he want to come home in time for my birthday? All that shit little kids say."

The wind rustled through the trees and dropped two dead leaves on Donovan's hood.

"I would never run away like this. No matter what happened. Did you kill somebody? 'Cause I don't think I would even run away then." Marcus shook his head. He thought for a moment, trying to conjure up something so horrible it would require living on top of the world. "Damn. When me and Jack started Uncle Roscoe's barn on fire, I knew I was gonna get beat. But I didn't run. I took it."

He glanced down at Main Street, where a lone car was driving by on the wrong side. Its only occupant slowed to view Donovan's new companion. Marcus stuck his middle fingers in the air, and his three friends laughed and did the same. The car sped off.

"Did you know my dad let Uncle Roscoe beat me too? After he was done with his damn belt, he hollered for Roscoe to come and take his turn. The ugly old fart comes in yelling and screaming about his expensive tools and how it took him six months to save up to buy them. I knew Grandma Bovant gave them to him after Grandpa Bovant died, but it wouldn't have done me no good to say so. My dad laughed while Roscoe used his belt on me."

Marcus sniffed, holding back tears. The last thing he needed was for his buddies to go home and tell his family he cried in public.

"Next day when Mom took me to the doctor, he said I broke three ribs. She told him I fell off my bike. How messed up is that? Did you have to explain your bruises too?"

Donovan brought his legs in closer to his chest. He wrapped his arms tightly around them, so tight the dry skin on his knuckles stretched uncomfortably. His jaw was clenched like he was suppressing a yawn. Marcus noticed for the first time the many lumps of foil sitting at the base of the tree. Several were labeled "for tree boy" or "a snack for you."

Like a wild animal hiding in the back yard, they were leaving bits of food and hoping he would sneak down during the night and grab them without being noticed. This was another part of the visit he would leave out. Telling them that Donovan was being fed like a stray dog would be too much. Grandma Bovant might take to her bed again and expect the grandkids to check on her during their lunch hours.

"Man, you stink. You're gonna get bugs in your head like Grandma's cat did. She died, last week, you know?" Donovan shifted at the mention of his grandmother. "No, man. Grandma didn't die. The cat. Myrtle or Turtle, whatever her name was."

Marcus allowed himself a brief glance at Donovan,

who was still staring intently at something that didn't exist. He felt a helplessness he had never experienced before. He just didn't understand what would make someone give up a warm bed for a tree branch. That's when he came up with a new plan.

Fred Baily, John Moran, and Luke Wright and Marcus lifted weights four days a week and despite the plethora of foiled items, Donovan looked like he hadn't eaten in a while. He was nothing but bones.

But then what?

Would anyone in Stanswick know how to fix him? His parents were so embarrassed, it was doubtful they would ever take him back unless and until he was close to normal. No one outside of the family would risk the ridicule that would come from taking him in.

"You ain't no shrink. Just knock him over the head and we'll catch him," Fred yelled impatiently. "Let's get out of this freak-hole."

"Luke, hand me the camera," Marcus instructed, ignoring Fred's outrageous suggestion.

"What?" Luke asked.

"Go get the camera and hand it up to me."

Luke ran to the pickup and retrieved his mom's camera. He kept it in the glove compartment in case he ever had a drunk cheerleader in the passenger seat and needed verification.

When he returned, Luke nimbly climbed up two branches and handed the camera to Marcus. "What're you gonna to do with that?" he asked. Lucas took the opportunity to stare at Donovan up close and touched his nose. Donovan didn't blink.

"Take his picture," Marcus replied, slapping Luke's hand away from his cousin's face.

"I thought we were takin' him home?"

When Marcus didn't reply, Luke sucked in a giant breath. "Oh, man. Are you going to sell pictures of your own cousin? That's cold."

"You can go now, Luke. I'll be down in a minute."

After Luke had descended, Marcus crouched in closer to Donovan, swallowing once and then breathing through his mouth to avoid foreign smells emanating from his cousin. He put one hand behind Donovan's head, making a peace sign with his fingers above Donovan's greasy hair and took a picture with the other. He felt guilty—a little, he would tell his friends later—but decided it was in Donovan's best interest to have his picture taken. When Donovan came to his senses the two of them would laugh about it, cousins hanging out in a tree.

As Marcus tilted the other direction to get a closer photo, he expected his sick cousin to look away in shame. Donovan, true to character, did not. His body remained frozen in much the same position it had been when their visit began.

"I'm leavin' you here, man," he said quietly. "You're too messed up for us. And this damn town is messed up too. You probably belong here." He got up and turned to climb back down the branch. "I'm keeping' the picture. For Sadie." he paused. "And your folks probably want to know you're okay." He knew this was an outright lie, but he felt he owed it to the boy who had shared so many Sunday afternoons with him in Grandma Bovant's back yard.

"Well, bye," he said uncomfortably. "Oh, and if you do ever decide to come home? That story about Uncle Roscoe? It ain't real." His face was crimson. "I made that up for you. You know he just gets a little hot when his things are broken. But I still wouldn't turn and run like a friggin' coward."

Marcus climbed down the tree, being careful to step around the various tin foil offerings. "What are you doin', man? You can't leave him here, can you?" John asked, incredulous.

"We didn't waste an entire case to drive here and not bring back the wrestling champ!" Fred echoed.

"I ain't takin' him. He's too crazy to live in my shed. What if he tries to kill himself? Don't want that on my conscience."

"It still seems wrong just to leave him." Luke shook his head. "Look at all of that food. They're probably drugging him for the sacrifice. He can live in their tree until he's good and fat, and then..."

Luke made a slicing motion across his neck.

"Look at him, jackass. He's just a bag of bones," Marcus snapped. "I doubt he's been down from that tree for more than a minute or two."

"Do you boys need some help?"

They all four turned to see a man dressed in some official garb standing beside a bicycle.

He was slowly, methodically gulping an RC Cola. When he finished, he stuck the bottle into some sort of holster in his belt loop and wiped his mouth with the back of his hand.

"Got a report that some young men were making offensive gestures to vehicles on Main Street. Would that be you, gentlemen?" He asked.

The boys laughed collectively at this—whoever he was—trying to bother them.

"It's hard to flip off more than one car when there is only one," Luke retorted. John and Fred both poked him in the side.

"Just scratching my nose, sir," Marcus responded politely. There was a snicker from one of his friends.

"Are you really a cop?" Luke asked. "I never seen a cop on a bike before."

They laughed collectively again.

"Like a cop for grade schoolers. Everyone else would run him over," One of the boys jeered.

Chief Blank chose to ignore the question. "Dag-blastit, I could fine you boys up to one hundred and fifteen dollars for making obscene gestures. And you did it at Elroy Evans, the oldest man in Pepperville. Didn't you learn to respect your elders?"

None of the boys replied nor did they care. They had pulled a lot of good pranks on people of all ages, they just hadn't gotten caught.

"We won't do it again, sir. We just came to see the freakshow." Luke gestured up to the tree, where Donovan remained motionless.

Chief Blank clucked his tongue in disapproval. "I can't do anything today since I didn't watch you committing the offense myself." His gaze moved to the fast food wrappers littering the ground beside each door of their truck.

"Sure could write you a ticket for litterin' though." The chief reached around to his back pocket and pulled out a brand new pad of tickets. To the left of his pop bottle was a smaller belt loop, with the long lid of a black pen hooked over the top. He pulled the pen out and began to write, left-handed, in a furious manner. "Now I don't usually write tickets when it's just a visitor. But I gotta be honest, you boys seem like trouble. Name?" He pointed his pen at Luke.

"Uhm.....officer, sir, we'll be glad to leave and never come back, if you just don't give us a ticket. My dad will ground me for a month if I come home with one-a-those things."

"Me too..." Marcus added. "Sir."

Chief Blank returned to his official document and continued scribbling furiously. All four of the boys had their hands in their pockets and swayed unsteadily from foot to foot while they waited.

Finally, Sean tore the ticket from its pad and handed it to Luke. "Now you see there, boys. I didn't fill in your names. That means as long as you pay the twenty-five dollar fine at my office before you leave town, there'll be no record of your time in Pepperville. My secretary is gone for the day, but there's envelopes in the mailbox. See that you leave your money sealed in there with your ticket and we'll be square."

John and Fred exchanged a smirk.

"There's no need to come to our fair city and harass folks. We put our shorts on one leg at a time, just like your kin."

When Luke snickered, he continued, "up a tree, down a drain, we don't care. We treat everyone like they're a long lost friend. Don't expect you to appreciate that at your tender age, but some day, you'll respect the town of Pepperville for that."

None of the still-inebriated boys seemed to care.

"On second thought, you boys need some time to figure things out. You're going to walk with me down to my office. I'll let you out when I think you've sobered up.

All four boys let out a cry of protest.

"Just remember, I do have your license plate number and a telephone to call the Stanswick station and get your names. And you," Chief Blank pointed at Marcus. "Next time your grandma comes to town, I could fill her ear with all sorts of stories, about your drinkin' and carousin' the streets of our fair city. I suspect she would be worked up in a good lather by the time she got home."

CHAPTER 17

Peter

P eter Reekblast had been stealing from his uncle for years. At first, it was just an "impulse-buy" trinket from beside the cash register. It was exhilarating to him; he had finally accomplished something without his mother, father, aunt, or uncle noticing. After a few months of coat pockets stuffed to overflowing with plastic flowers and *Have a Great Day!* pins, he found the process had lost its allure.

One day, his Uncle Fenderson was bemoaning the fact that his mint julep fudge was not selling as it should. He told Peter to make sure and push it, even going so far as to offer a free piece with every purchase over ten dollars. After he left, Peter eyed the sixteen pans of fudge carefully. He could take a few pieces from each pan and no one would notice. He could eat them or, better yet, sell them to his buddies after school. Sure would be better than the lousy $3.50 an hour he was making now, and he wouldn't have to sweep up when he finished.

He stuck a piece from each pan in his pocket and then looked around, sure that his uncle's booming voice would catch him off guard. But the room was silent. He took a few more. The next day, after repackaging each piece in plastic wrap, he sold every bit of candy from his backpack. Peter wasn't stupid; he realized that he couldn't empty the pans every time he worked. But eventually, his locker became a booming black market for fudge of sixteen flavors.

He began to eat his anxiety and, at the same time, his small profit margin. Peter started gaining weight, and although his uncle did not notice the missing items, his parents began to suspect he had other issues.

His mother insisted he see a therapist twice a week until his weight problem was resolved. Both of his parents were in agreement that a boy who didn't participate in sports must be touched in the head. While they supported his efforts to earn extra money (via his uncle's store), they felt that his overeating must be a product of too much stored energy and a need for a more vigorous outlet. So Peter trudged to the one therapist in town, seventeen-and-a-half blocks from school, twice weekly.

Public outings in Pepperville just plain did not go unnoticed. Everyone in high school knew about Peter's "problem." Everyone in his parents' social circle also had some idea. The rumors spread until it was widely accepted that Peter had threatened to impale a customer at Flowers, Flowers, and Fudge on a potted cactus. Business that week was down dramatically. But the next week, people had pretty much forgotten about it or decided their flower and candy needs were too great to avoid the business.

The therapist diagnosed Peter as "unusually angry" and "very bored" and prescribed a strict exercise regimen of three miles around the high school track every morning, as well as positive thinking tapes from Calley and more vegetables.

There was the usual ribbing from his classmates, and giggling and eye rolling from the girls. No one bought fudge from him anymore because they had heard rumors from their parents that he was disturbed. And of course, everyone in high school, including the janitor knew that he was seeing the therapist.

One day, Peter could take it no more. It was during Familiar Literature 101. The book for this month's class was *Forget Not the Whales* by Horatio Winestaff. Although the whales in the story were merely a euphemism for those larger than life in deeds and writings, the class took this opportunity to attack Peter's weight gain.

One student, the star player on the basketball team, taped Peter's school picture from last fall to the cover of the book and left it in the middle of the chalkboard. There was snickering throughout the class and poor Peter had to endure it without complaint for the entire hour. To tattle would have made him an even bigger target. The teacher saw the book as the bell rang and removed it immediately, but the offending student had already left the room.

It was only 11:37 a.m., but Peter could stand it no more. He ran all the way home, three quarters of a mile. He ran up the back stairs and into his bedroom, where he sobbed silently in his pillow for close to twenty minutes.

When all of the tears had been produced that could be, Peter lay with his face in the pillow trying to decide what to do next. It was at this point that he realized someone else was in the house. There were muffled sounds coming from his sister's room right next to his, but he was sure she wouldn't skip school. She was only in second grade, and the thought probably hadn't even occurred to her yet.

He listened further and realized that there were two voices and they were both familiar. He reached down beside his bed and grabbed the half-empty glass of soda off the plate of cookies and chips from his midnight cupboard raid of the night before. He gulped the last of the liquid and wiped it out with his hand.

Peter placed the glass up against the wall and strained to listen. The voices were happy, almost euphoric. He could only make out every third or fourth word: "like it....my house...next...she would...."

It was at this point that he realized the female voice he heard was that of his aunt Winnie.

She had a distinct, high-pitched nasal sound when she was happy or excited. He put the glass down and walked to his door. He had his hand on the knob when he realized that the other voice in his sister's room was that of his father. Peter fell to his floor and sat, staring at his messy room. He heard more distinct sounds now like they were doing something he didn't want to think about. In his sister's room. On his sister's bed.

Peter had to get out of his own house then, before he found himself in the awkward situation of catching his aunt and his father in the throes of passion while he was skipping school. More than dealing with the hurt of this event, he wanted to get out of his house undetected.

He opened his door slowly, pulling ever-so-slightly on the doorknob so that the hinges didn't make their usual squeak. He crawled on his hands and knees down the stairs and did not stand until he reached the back door. When he was finally outside, he let out a *whoosh* of air and realized he had been holding his breath this entire time.

Relieved to escape unnoticed, he ran around the front of the house to his driveway, but by that time the reality of his awful life had set in and he had to stop to throw up all over the chalk drawings of giant sunshines his sister had created just yesterday.

There was no time to stand on ceremony; he desperately needed to leave. As soon as his shaky knees would carry him, he got up and ran. He ran up and down every side street on the way and did not pause until he reached Main Street. By now, the hurt in him had crawled up through his generous stomach, sliding up his throat until it grabbed him around the neck and began to choke him. He had to stop and try to breathe.

Peter bent over, hands on knees, and sucked in big gulps of the cool, fall air. It hurt to breathe. He pushed the image of his father and his aunt as far from his mind as he could. He pushed out the sounds, and the thought of his sister's bed, now unfit for her to sleep in. Finally, he felt composed enough to stand. He just happened to be standing in front of the tree – Donovan's tree.

Donovan was gazing at the traffic and had not noticed the dire condition of Peter Reekblast. Donovan's only concern seemed to be the stick he was using to scrape at the tree branch underneath his feet. He sat almost motionless, one hand over his knees and the other methodically scraping.

For some reason, this infuriated Peter. "Hey!" he called. "Freak! Hey you!" Donovan glanced at him but made no attempt to respond. "I'm talking to you! You're a worthless piece of crap! What kind of freakin' animal sits on a branch all day? You think you're better than us?"

Peter yelled. "I just heard my dad and my aunt— and you hide like a baby because of one wrestling match?"

Somehow he expected more satisfaction from this conversation. He wanted Donovan to feel the pain and humiliation that was coursing through his own body. He put his hands in his pockets and felt the fudge that had been sitting there all week. It was rock hard. He took out the first piece, Mocha la Rumba, and hurled it at Donovan. It hit the platform he was sitting on and bounced off.

Peter moved around toward the street, so that he was squarely facing Donovan. He took out the discolored rock that was once Peanut Butter Passion and aimed again. This time, it hit Donovan's foot. The next several pieces came in rapid-fire motion. Donovan did not try and escape the attack. One hit his arm, then his cheek, then another on his ear. It was as if he invited the abuse. Several pieces scratched his skin.

When Peter ran out of fudge, he turned to whatever was conveniently located around his feet. First, it was sticks, then rocks, then a broken pop bottle. By now there was blood trickling down Donovan's face from several wounds. Still, he said nothing. Peter had run out of objects within his immediate location and started kicking the tree. He kicked it so hard the branches began to shake.

"Dag-blastit, boy! Why're you so dead set on hurtin' someone?" Chief Blank had ridden up behind him and now grabbed Peter by the arms.

"You okay up there, son?" He looked up at Donovan but quickly returned his focus to the resistant boy in his grasp. The normally well-pressed and neatly presented officer spilled pop on his khaki shorts while trying to dismount his bike and look up at the same time. The strands of hair covered in styling gel, and at one point placed firmly on the right side of his head were now hanging loosely about his face. His calm demeanor belied the disheveled, middle-aged man standing in front of Peter. And yet, he was in control.

After several minutes of struggle, Peter realized it was no use and he sunk into Chief Blank's firm grip. His shoulders rounded in surrender, and he stared hard at the ground.

"Donovan, you need some medical assistance, boy?"

The tree dweller wiped his bloody face on the sleeve of his jacket and turned, still sitting on his haunches ape-style, to face the street. He glanced back ever-so-slightly to eyeball the lumberjack shirt Charlotte O'Cann had tossed up on her mail rounds last Sunday evening. Donovan reached back without looking and grabbed the shirt. He pushed his entire face into the green and yellow plaid, and sat posed like that for several minutes.

Chief Blank was growing tired of standing in wet pants, and even more so of strong-arming this delinquent while he waited for Donovan to make up his mind. "Last call, son. I'll get you some help if you want it."

"He's stupid or somethin'. Even my dog talks more than him," Peter taunted, shifting his eyes between the lunchtime high school traffic that was filling the streets and the ground. Sean twisted Peter's collar just enough to send a message. His bicep bulged as he held this position.

"All right, Donovan. I'll leave you alone for now,

but folks'll be concerned. You need to prepare yourself."

Turning to Peter, he changed his tone one of disgust. "Let's git you home, or at least your dad's office. He isn't goin' to be happy about this."

Peter wondered if his father and his Aunt Winnie had even left his house. *This would teach them.*

CHAPTER 18

Jenna

She had led those boys straight to Donovan. Chances were good that he had been hiding from someone like this, and if Jenna were a better person, a more compassionate person, she might help him. But this was a small town and they would find him sooner or later.

Jenna imagined Donovan cut to bits and lying on the side of the road, all because of her directions. A pack of dogs and cats would be fighting over his leftovers. The long, brown coat would lie beside the road for months, becoming tatters and eventually bits of anonymous fabric blown into the next county on a windy day. There would be nothing to remind them that Donovan Bovant once existed, and the deepest, darkest part of her felt some sick satisfaction.

Her mother's death had been equally unceremonious. There had been no goodbye. Every book she read as a child, especially the fairy tales, included the dramatic death of one of the main characters. But they had all said their goodbyes; imparted one last secret; kissed the cheek of the one person who would miss them the most.

Jenna had come in from washing Drake Ashton's car that Saturday afternoon. Even though he hadn't driven it since high school, it was important that all of the property maintain a certain appearance. She was going to ask her mother for the two hundredth time if she could please, please have one of her own. She had taken driver's education in the tenth grade and had even gotten her driver's permit. Her mother always argued that Pepperville was small enough that they could walk wherever they needed to go. A car was just one more expense they simply didn't need.

It was the suffocating noonday sun that had sparked Jenna's plan. She would offer to help the groundskeeper for two dollars an hour. All of the other girls in her class had suntans, and she wanted one, too. After she earned enough for a down payment (how-ever much that would be), she and her mother could pick out something small and practical. She would park it down the street even, not on Ashton property. There was no way her mother could turn her down because she wasn't asking for much more than her permission.

Jenna bounded in the back door of Ashton Mansion, the one by the kitchen, not caring if her wet feet left marks on the floor. She knocked on the door of her mother's room, and when she didn't receive a reply, she decided, brazenly, to scour the kitchen for a suitable snack item.

It would be thirty minutes more before Jenna returned to the door, apple in hand. She had become distracted by the disorderly state of the drawers in the kitchen and decided to set them right, something she knew would please her mother. This time she opened it impatiently when her mother didn't answer.

There, lying on the bed, hands neatly folded on her chest, was her mother; her short brown hair splayed out on the pillow and her maid's uniform maintained its starched appearance. Her matching gray shoes, the ones she had found in a medical supply catalog, were placed beside the bed as if she had paused only to rest for a few minutes. But her lips were blue, and they parted in an unnaturally lazy way that did not look like the mother she knew. Jenna touched her mother's arm and found it to be uncomfortably cool.

"I'll get you a blanket, Mom," she said robotically. She stepped out and shut the door, slowly coming to the realization that something was wrong. Jenna stepped back in and touched her mother again. It was too much to fully comprehend.

"You need your shoes on, Mom," she said weakly. Jenna grabbed a gray shoe and tried to stuff her mother's foot into it. Something was wrong. The shoe was too small.

Jenna threw it against the wall and began pacing in a circle. Her mother wouldn't leave her like this; the punishment was far too severe for the minor crime of wanting something they couldn't afford. Or maybe her mother had been planning this since the embarrassment of her birthday party? If it hadn't been for Jenna, Mrs. Ashton would not have exposed herself in front of so many common people. Her secret life of alcohol and misery would have died with her. All because a simple girl wanted a cake and balloons.

Jenna had humiliated her own mother by forcing her to share her complicated life of caregiver and servant with a bunch of grade school girls. Maybe that was why her mother had kept this from her, knowing Jenna would create another public spectacle. She planned her death, her private passing, specifically while her daughter was out of the house. Now there would be no way to apologize for the request for frivolity, a car like her wealthier classmates possessed. Where would she have driven anyway?

"No...NO...NO..NO!" she repeated. It was several minutes before she thought about the possibility of her mother being saved. She ran across the considerable lawn and out the front gate, its ivory "A" banging precariously in the wind. The first human being she found happened to be Greg Prembone, Anessa's hapless older brother. Jenna's heart sunk.

Greg was walking his dog in front of the Ashton property and when Jenna sobbed that her mother wasn't responsive, he came without hesitation. He had read several handouts on medical resuscitation and was confident he could help. As he tied his dog to a tree and trotted to rejoin Jenna, he recited the first aid essentials he had retained.

"I can do CPR. It's like kissin' someone only the opposite. Breathin' out instead of in. You shoulda come to that class, Jenna. I got a brochure at home that explains it real good." He spoke breathlessly.

Jenna did not reply.

"I saw this video on burns in that class too. You sure don't want to put butter on them things. That's what Grandma told me to do, but it makes it worse..."

When they reached the bedroom, Greg's face turned white. He had never seen a dead person before. He had witnessed the death of several pets and more than a few frying-chickens, but this was of a different nature entirely.

He was quite sure disease and infection could overtake them any second. For a brief moment, he pictured himself as the brave hero, picking up Jenna's mother and handing her to the volunteer fire chief, Chief Blank. But this wasn't the way people looked in the videos; stiff and lifeless. There was no air moving in the room. He started feeling little dizzy.

"Jenna, your mama's gone," he said quietly. "There ain't nothin' I can do."

Jenna stood, arms crossed in the doorway. She wasn't moving, nor was she showing any signs of acknowledgment.

"If you want, I'll go get the doctor. He can confirm. She probably just laid down to take a rest and never woke up. My grandpa did that too. It's the best way to go," Greg said. He looked at the frail girl, the one who did her best to remain unnoticed. She was hugging her waist so tightly it was possible she wanted to stop breathing herself. Greg's Dachshund, tied to one of the massive oaks on the Ashton property, was barking furiously at a passing squirrel.

"Just sit yourself down, Jenna. Me an' Flex will go get the doctor and be right back."

"NO! I'll get the doctor. It's my mom. You go on home."

Greg tried to force Jenna into the chair, but she resisted. Greg wasn't a fighter but certainly was not prepared for this kind of nightmare. Finally, he pushed her to a squatting position, which was good enough for him.

The minute he walked out, closing the door behind him, Jenna stood up defiantly. As she glanced once more at her mother's lifeless body, the memory of Mrs. Ashton's dead body and the overwhelming smells flooded into her brain.

Expensive liquor combined with a stale, ugly odor her mother would later inform was the process of the soul leaving the body, filled the Maroon Room. Her mother removed the urine-stained nightgown and dressed Mrs. Ashton in a pale, blue sweater with matching polyester pants.

"You can fix her hair. Make it look nice before the mortician arrives. She wouldn't want to appear unkempt for visitors."

Jenna was frightened and wanted her mother to

take her into another room and hold her tightly until this first image of death left her mind. But she was also brave and brave girls didn't let on when they were terrified.

"Go ahead. You can use this opportunity to tell her goodbye. Thank her for taking care of us." Her mother picked up a laundry basket full of Mrs. Ashton's dirty things matter-of-factly, the way she handled all crises regarding the household. Her face bore no hint of sadness or regret, nor did she seem especially pleased that she would sleep in her bed without fear of 2:00 a.m. phone calls from a drunken woman.

Jenna's head was spinning. She was horrified. But the longer she sat, the more a sense of power overtook her. She was finally alone with the great Mrs. Ashton, able to say or do whatever she wished without fear.

A sterling silver engraved brush with the letters *MA* sat on the nightstand. There were several strands of gray hair entwined within its shiny bristles. Hairs that came off a warm, living human being. Now the old woman's hair was knotted and twisted on the pillow. It looked as if it had desperately tried to escape her body before her death.

Jenna stared at the old, worn face; tight, yellow skin. Her nostrils, so tiny and pinched that they often made a delicate whistling sound when Mrs. Ashton breathed. There was no sound emanating from them now.

Jenna picked up the brush and held it in her hand. She considered making the woman look truly hideous, but she couldn't bring herself to disappoint her mother. The brush glided through the knotty hair with surprising ease. She remembered her mother had washed it just yesterday, probably in preparation for the old woman's death. (Her mother had a knack for planning ahead.)

When she felt it was sufficiently tamed, she set the brush back on the nightstand, relieved the process of brushing the hair of a dead person hadn't been more traumatic.

"I hate you," she said quietly. It felt powerful. "I hate you!" she said again, louder and with more confidence. "You're an awful, mean woman and no one will miss you. Not me, or my mother!"

Something on the nightstand caught her eye, something shiny and beautiful. It was a pair of glittery, diamond earrings, each one the size of a penny. She remembered the many parties hosted by the Ashton family. Mrs. Ashton, with hair upswept, would swing a cigarette around as if she were using it to conduct an orchestra while she spoke in an animated fashion.

The other hand contained a cocktail of some kind that always gave off the odor of an over-chlorinated swimming pool. Those magnificent orbs (acquired by Mr. Ashton while on a hunting expedition in Africa) sagged from her earlobes almost touching her narrow shoulders; sparkling exclamation points to end each dramatic sentence she used.

After each party, they had been carefully wrapped and stored in the family safe. Now they sat so carelessly in the open, where any staff member could touch and scrutinize them.

Jenna gingerly lifted them, trying to imagine the exotic life they led in faraway Africa before coming to reside on the ears of such a distasteful and boring old woman. She tried visualizing beautiful exotic women trying them on and then putting them back, in favor of something even more wondrous. And now they would glisten from the ears of the downstairs maid, who had eyed them hungrily ever since working her first formal party. There was no doubt the staff would ravage through this bedroom as soon as her mother's back was turned, claiming every memento in sight.

"Jenna, are you finished yet? I need you to listen for the mortician downstairs," her mother called. Without thinking, she grabbed the earrings and stuffed them in the pocket of her jeans.

Several hours later, she hid them under the bed in the maid's bedroom planning to retrieve them when she was fully grown. She would tell her mother they were something she bought, some second-hand trinket to use just for her wedding. Hopefully, by that time, her mother would have forgotten all about the missing diamonds.

For several months she felt anxiety over the theft, but when the Ashton boys swooped in to protect their family's treasures from the "unscrupulous" population of Pepperville, not one word was mentioned about the missing earrings.

There were more pressing details to attend to at

that point. It was common knowledge that the old lady hated her stepsons with a passion. The boys never once visited after their father died, and some say Mrs. Ashton felt abandoned by everyone but her staff.

Ten employees, mostly just there for show and not doing any substantial work, scaled down from thirty in the mansion's heyday, retained their stiff uniforms in anticipation of the eventual passing of the grand dame of the property. Rumors flew from the mouths of those who had been in attendance when Mrs. Ashton called her attorney into the musty study to revise her will. The miserly woman was leaving everything to her loyal employees—those who remained until the end.

Even Jenna, from a tender age, had heard the stories though she never dared consult her mother to see if they were true. Her mother had a genuine fondness for the mistress and wouldn't approve of her daughter gossiping about her demise.

Of course, in the end, she left all of her worldly goods to the boys. The meetings with her lawyer had been more of a social call than anything. She was lonely. The tea and cookies in anticipation of an alleged change in her will were her way of forcing him to remain in her presence.

When the boys learned that the employees had been pilfering family goods, all but Jenna and her mother were fired, without severance pay. Jenna's mother was asked to stay on to oversee the mansion property, as much as a favor to the unskilled woman and her young daughter as it was a way to keep the property well maintained in their absence.

Eventually, Jenna forgot about the existence of the earrings. Something that had once seemed so important became meaningless for many years. Until this horrible day.

Underneath the bed, in the formal maid's room, a yellowed sweat sock still contained the glittering earrings. They were just as perfect as Jenna remembered. As she picked them up, she realized they were made for pierced ears. Neither Jenna nor her mother had ever worn jewelry, and their ears were free of piercings.

She went to the kitchen and opened all of the drawers. Not much remained from the impressive collection of pots, pans, knives, and flatware once utilized in the busy mansion kitchen. She found a small paring knife and returned to her mother's bedroom. Was her mother looking more at peace, or had Jenna just gotten used to staring at a lifeless body, the one that used to contain the person she held so dear?

Carefully she pricked tiny spaces in her mother's ears, trying to make the holes as big as she had observed on the girls at school. She pulled each earring through and stood back to admire her work.

There was a second sensation of shock that day. Her mother looked glamorous. She could have been the beautiful socialite, dining with the rich and bored on a ridiculously large boat.

Jenna took her mother's hands and placed them carefully on top of one another so that she looked like a princess in repose. Jenna took some satisfaction from the scene. Her mother had finally become the picture of sophistication her daughter had always dreamed she should be. And beyond that, she deserved something for her years of service to this property.

She gazed at her only known relative for one more minute, and then closed the door to her mother's room. There, by the back door were her red, rubber boots. They felt comfortable and familiar on her feet.

She spent the night sitting in the darkness of her closet in the little cottage. It was around noon the next day when her high school French teacher forced her way into the house and pulled Jenna from the closet. She tried at first to gently coax her. Realizing that her attempts at communication were unsuccessful, she said nothing further but took Jenna by her arms and walked her into the other room and phoned Doctor Franz.

The doctor arrived eventually with some kind of sedative, just to calm her down, he said. Like sitting in a catatonic state in that dark space all night wasn't about all the calm a human being could handle.

Jenna continued her journey of isolation much the way it had begun; all by herself in the gray-blue cottage behind the big mansion. Her life became a series of monotonous routines meant to keep her alive while allowing her to die inside a little each day.

Lots of folks tried politely to help but she refused

any assistance and was only seen in public when she had to be. It was understandable that she would need an opportunity to breathe before facing the storm of sympathetic head-nodders, eyes filled with pity.

Too bad someone like me didn't step in. At least I owed her that.

CHAPTER 19

Grandma Bovant

A nessa hugged her warmly. "I haven't seen you for so long, Grandma Bovant! Have you been away?"

"No, child. I haven't been travelin'." She studied Anessa's face, it was smooth and shiny and almost as pretty as one of her favorite granddaughters.

Since her thoughts were elsewhere, it took her a minute to comprehend the change in complexion. "You've got yourself a young man now, don't you? A local one?"

"Yeah, I have a *boyfriend*." That word, new to Anessa's vocabulary, came out easily and without her usual boastful attitude. He's even good-lookin', for an older man, that is." She smiled slyly.

"What?" Grandma Bovant clucked her tongue in mock disgust. "Now you didn't go and find yourself a married one, did you? If so, I'll need to sit you down for a good talk."

"No, it's Chief Blank. Look—we're pearled now." She stuck out her hand displaying a giant pearl surrounded by four synthetic pink tourmalines, her birthstone.

"Oh my," Grandma Bovant said, doing her best to appear impressed. "Just one step away from the diamond then. Good girl. You're on the right track." She looked at the floor. "Well, I s'pose you know why I'm here."

"Your usual? There should be plenty on aisle—"

"No, I got that here." She sat a box on the counter. "I come for the boy. Where is he?"

Anessa's face reddened.

"I'm ashamed, Anessa. If I'da known, I'da been here long ago. But how could I? I'da come, that's for sure. That's not how we raised him. He had a real future in the wrestling."

This was a curious state of affairs: Grandma had already crowned Marcus to be Donovan's successor in all extracurricular sports and academics. But one burning issue remained: how would she explain to her bridge club that she had been such a complete failure when it came to the boy she christened the Blond Jesus?

There had been rumors all over town, and by now most people knew that Donovan was in the middle of a breakdown of some sort. If she couldn't talk him down, she would have to cut him out of her life permanently, as the rest of the Bovants had done.

"Oh, you're here about Donovan." Anessa smiled.

"We've been takin' real good care of him. He's like one of us now."

Anessa turned the key to shut off her register and guided Grandma Bovant outside and across the street. She explained the containers left beneath the tree and made a point of saying out that Phyliss Dorlock set out an entire apple pie.

Even though she parked her car not far from the tree and walked right by it as she went into the store, Grandma Bovant had been completely oblivious to his presence.

"Feedin' him like a dog." She let out a disgusted sigh when Vanessa finished a detailed description of each package. Grandma Bovant didn't like charity and she was even more ashamed that Donovan took leftovers from all of these unfamiliar people with such relative ease. She picked up several foil packages and little notes of encouragement and put them in her purse.

"Oh, no. There's more than food. People have been leavin' all sorts of things. You know, to wish him well." Anessa grabbed an ornately decorated note with something taped to the back and handed it to Mrs. Bovant.

Luckily, the print on the last one was large enough she could read it without her special glasses:

Only you know why you're in the tree. Our entire congregation is praying for your safe return to ground level.

God Bless,
The Reekblast Family

Taped to the back of the note was a cross, crocheted in gold yarn. At that moment, she understood. She felt a twinge of guilty pride; all these years she had been telling people that Donovan was the Chosen One. Now here he was, up on the Mount, waiting for his Sign.

In the meantime, strangers from all walks of life had made pilgrimages to see her boy, placing offerings at his feet. She looked up at him and caught a shock of blond hair underneath his dark brown hood. He was the icon she always knew he would become, and she was right here to witness. His first prophetic words would be to the woman he loved more than his own mother. She could feel it.

Grandma Bovant took a deep breath and stuck her chest out. He wasn't there to embarrass her at all. He was going to save the world, thanking his granny for her years of guidance at every turn. Just as soon as he came down from the tree.

"Donovan, honey?" she said in an innocent voice. She heard rustling, but no sign of the face of her favorite grandchild. "Sweet boy, Granny needs to talk to you. Can you come over to this side of the tree, please?" She knew him well enough to understand how much she meant to him. She'd just have to be patient.

To her surprise, he moved to the side of his platform facing her.

"I ain't gonna lie to you. We all knew you was here. Marcus says he tried talkin' you down and you wasn't about to do it. Said he told you we was all missin' you.

Well that ain't all true. Your daddy don't let nobody talk about you anymore, so Marcus had to come to me in the middle of the night. I was in my best pink nightie and rollers, but Marcus said it was important and it was about you."

Grandma paused, wondering if he'd lost his hearing and she should drive over to Bill's Hardware and find herself a bull horn.

"Keep going!" Anessa encouraged.

"I figured you was where you wanted to be. Young people always have their fits of crazy. But then that lawyer showed up at the door with a note. Don't nobody need to come to my house and bring me letters 'bout my own kin. He wouldn't tell me who'd been writin', but it was someone who wanted you down. They says, 'Come and get your boy.'"

Anessa put one hand on her chest. "Who would do something so awful?" she asked in horror.

Grandma Bovant frowned at Anessa, tired of an audience. At this point, she supposed she didn't have a choice in the matter.

"Granny understands. You have a higher callin'. You're here to git The Message." She smiled a smile of self-satisfaction that she alone had solved this mystery. "Don't you want to talk to me though? Tell me about your visions?"

No response.

"No, I don't s'pose you can. 'til it's the right time." She blushed, angry with herself for forgetting there was a process to these things. Then again, her plan was to bring Donovan home, the only one in the family capable of such a task.

What are you gonna do, Leona? Are you strong enough in your faith to wait for the boy to find his sign, or do you need the family to admire you?

Visions or not, he was going to have to come down and face her so she could examine him for signs of illness.

"I can get that nice policeman to help you down. Just so's you can say hi to Granny."

"Oh, he won't come. This is when he lifts weights." The voice was Anessa's, once again piping up when she wasn't needed. Grandma Bovant eyed her sternly, trying to convey that it was time for Anessa to exit.

Then she realized that Anessa's presence was a way to document this experience, confirming her title as Grandmother to the Prophet.

"Anessa, darlin,' come pray with Granny. Let's give Donovan a reason to show us his face." She reached out her hand to Anessa.

"I don't know anything about praying," she replied.

"I'll show you," Grandma insisted, wiggling her hand insistently. As soon as the girl was within reach, she grabbed Anessa's hand and pulled her into her cushiony side. "Dear Lord..." she began.

"Dear....God," Anessa feebly tried to mimic Grandma's words.

"I know you lifted my boy. You lifted him up so high that now he can't get down." Grandma's eyes were pressed tightly together but she could sense a crowd forming on the sidewalk behind her.

"You...li...li...lifted high...ground..." Anessa tried following unsuccessfully.

"Bring him down to eye-level now." She tried mimicking the sound of her favorite pastor in a sing-song voice that resonated through the entire church, raise both of their hands above her head. "Part the twigs and leaves, and set him right here in front of his granny so he can give me his message. And while you're workin' on him, Lord, I know you remembered to take out all the crazy that comes from his mother's side. Amen."

"Amen."

A burst of applause erupted from the people who unexpectedly had stumbled upon a miracle. Of what sort, they weren't sure. But there was a car with out-of-town license plates, and someone was saying a blessing on Main Street, so it had to be a monumental experience.

There had been no movement from Donovan; no reaction whatsoever. Those observing wondered if this was meant to be an obvious slight to his grandmother, which would have been unforgivable to them.

Leona, while pleased she'd attracted a crowd, still felt unsatisfied. She had to find something tangible to return with or the family wouldn't believe she'd been there. Her revelation that her grandson was a Chosen One would not be enough to convince the family that he was of sound mind and perfectly acceptable right where he was; she would need words of confirmation at the very least.

"Don't you want to say anything to me, son? I've come all this way."

"If you've come asking for something, you'll need to cleanse your own soul first," someone from the crowd offered.

Grandma shook her head.

"I don't know what else to say to you, son. I've tried sweet-charmin' and we've got a pretty girl down here, there's nothin' let for me to...." She paused and looked down at her man-sized, farm-worn hands. Clasped between her fingers was a sack containing a fifty-year-old secret.

"Grandbaby, I'm gonna tell you a secret and then you can do me a favor, okay? Do you know why I make all of these trips to Pepperville? Do you remember all of those times you came with Granny, and we did ourselves proud at the ice cream shop after we went shoppin'?" She paused, hoping again for some response from him. There was none. "I was buyin' this."

She pulled a box, slowly and dramatically, from the brown paper bag she was holding. There, on the front of the box was the picture of an attractive, auburn-haired woman. Above her head were the words, Fountain of Youth, Red Devil Number Seven.

"It's hard to believe, son, but this is my red hair, right here in this box. I'm no more a red-headed Bovant than you are."

She let out a sigh of relief. It was finally out in the

open after all these years of 3:00 a.m. washings. Even after her husband died, she continued her covert operations; partly for the thrill of being up at that hour with a purpose, and partly because the older she got the more paranoid she became. It wasn't beyond her scope of possibilities that an errant Bovant would end up in her yard in the middle of the night; out of gas or sick and needing medical attention.

She felt proud of herself: proud that she had finally confessed to someone that she had been dying her hair, and proud that she had thought of a way to connect with Donovan. "My hair used to be the color of dirty water. It was just plain ugly. When I saw your granddaddy for the first time, I knew I was going to marry him." She touched her beehive of red curls unconsciously.

"My family had just moved to Stanswick from back East, so no one knew me. I found out everything I could about Granddad. Didn't take long before I realized I'd need to do more than bat my eyelashes. I figured if I was gonna be a Bovant, I'd have to look the part. So I started dyin' my hair.

Granddaddy never knew. Never even asked why my roots was sometimes a little different than the rest of my head. Can you imagine? He was none too bright, your granddad, but he milked a cow like nobody's business," she continued. "That's why me an' Anessa here at the Shoppe and Walke know each other so well. She's a sweet thing. She'd be a good match for you, hon." She nodded her head as if encouraging him to speak. "No one ever asked me, and I never told. It's been the best-kept family secret."

Donovan stared in her general direction, not blinking for several minutes. Instead of having the desired effect on him, he looked as if he had been poked in the heart once again.

One can only imagine his feelings after hearing that all of those special trips he made with her were purely for *her* benefit. She hadn't been taking him out of town just because he was someone special; someone who deserved to be loved. He sat alone in Fudge, Fudge and Flowers, eating his piece of walnut and peanut butter fudge each time. "Granny's gonna run a quick errand. You'll be all right by yourself then?"

She touched her hair and kissed him on the head. Every time.

It was his last connection to his family, and he was watching it crumble before his eyes. He moved back to his previous branch, sitting on his haunches with his arms around his knees.

The people watching had lost interest and moved on, and even Anessa had returned to her check stand. Grandma Bovant was left alone on the ground, with her favorite grandson perched above her.

No one in the family had actually disobeyed her or even said the word "no" to her; at least not since her mother-in-law passed away, and that was back when she could still fit into her wedding dress. Whatever Granny wanted, she got. It was she who decided which boys would become wrestling stars. She chose

Donovan to be in the center mat and had even decided where she would buy his first home after he graduated from State University.

While Anessa was a cute prospect and would have been a nice distraction, in reality, Grandma Bovant had already chosen a girl: a pretty red-head from Stanswick who would accompany him to college and make the perfect mate. All of Granny's sons, grandsons, and a few nephews had turned out exactly as she had intended; and even the boys working in the meat packing plant were content with their lives.

She lost two children shortly after birth, but neither loss had been quite so painful as this moment right now. The support of every single relative in Stanswick eased that pain. She had no one now.

She decided against retrieving the sheriff. Grandma Bovant would have to leave town carrying only a package of Fountain of Youth, Red Devil Number Seven and fragments of her dignity. Even at that, she paused when she reached her car and turned around hopefully.

"You'll come home once you get the message. I know that's how it works, son. I just have to be patient."

She hoisted her oversized body into the car and lifted her voluminous breasts above the seatbelt. She had herself the first big cry she had allowed since the death of her husband, some fourteen years earlier. How could the boy she loved and practically raised be so cruel and heartless? Not even a hug?

Grandma Bovant told him her most guarded secret, and he had nothing to say in response. She had shown him more sympathy than the rest of the family who erased his name from the "births" column in the family Bible on the second week of his absence. She was a good grandmother—the best—she told herself as she drove away.

As she saw things, the stories of divine inspiration would have to wait for his miraculous return when he would tell them himself. Despite the fact that she was sure it would happen soon, she couldn't say anything to anyone. She possessed only a few crumpled notes and stale leftovers that she knew her sons would scoff at. Her faith was being tested, and now was the time to stand silently, no matter what the neighbors and her family thought.

In her rear-view mirror (the one she wasn't watching), Donovan was crying visibly as well. Not just crying, but *sobbing*. Big, loud, whooping sobs like an injured animal.

CHAPTER 20

Jenna

I t had been three months since Donovan found his tree perch in Pepperville.

Obviously, the bones left under the tree had not been a success and Jenna felt guilt over the fact that the poor girl was now missing a bone.

Jenna had to come up with another plan—a sure thing. While murder never crossed her mind up to that point in her life, one of the Ashton's rifles and a well-placed bullet did occur to her as a way to solve her problems instantly.

But that wasn't the Jenna everyone knew and tolerated, if not outright loved. Instead, she would find another way to drive this interloper from his comfortable perch. So far, the answer was unclear.

She obsessed over it while she cleaned and while she ate. Jenna thought about getting rid of him as she drifted off to sleep. It was the first thing that came to her mind, as she was brushing her teeth every morning.

It was so much easier than confronting her own problems.

One day while in Calley's studio, she came up with an ingenious idea. Calley was not concerned for her own privacy and left many personal items in her aerobics studio in plain sight.

Since Calley believed all medication should be taken at precisely 10:00 a.m. every morning (*Love Your Life, Love Your Meds, 1982)*, those currently in use, as well as long ago expired medications, sat on top of the microwave in the storage closet/snack area.

Jenna was certainly not stupid, but she was also unsure of the intended use for the round package labeled as birth control pills. One thing was certain: They were medication and as such, they would pose a threat to someone for whom they had not been prescribed.

A container, marked "hummus dip, serve with carrots and potato chips," sat innocently on the top shelf of the refrigerator. Jenna removed the Tupperware lid and a pungent aroma assaulted her nose. Judging by the brown lumps, some sort of a bean was included in this recipe.

She took another sniff. Cumin, and a vinegar smell. Was the mystery ingredient in this week's FFAF some sort of bottled salad dressing? An odd Italian variety with too many spices? This was too easy.

She would tell Calley it slipped from her hands as she was cleaning the refrigerator. A likely scenario, but that would require her to admit to removing the lid to judge the contents. She would tell her she was only sampling, as Calley had encouraged her to do those many weeks after her mother's death when she couldn't bring herself to enter the Shoppe and Walke, or anywhere else for that matter.

Could she really do this?

It wouldn't kill him, she reasoned, just make him sick enough to come down from that tree, and then Officer Blank would ride beside him as he walked to the city limits. Everyone would be so relieved when he was gone and life returned to normal!

She was sure she was righting a wrong and the container, along with the offensive smelling dip, made the trip back to her kitchen for further preparation.

Jenna mashed the pills with her fingers until there was nothing left but powder and then carefully integrated it with the lumps of beans. She stepped back several times to eye her creation. Finally, she deemed the product a "normal" consistency. It would sit on the counter unrefrigerated, final pièce de resistance, until she finished cleaning.

Jenna fantasized about another way to remove him from his perch after returning home with her mixture. Bow and arrow. She was sure Anessa had spoken of Greg's passion for shooting at things with arrows. Maybe, she thought, he could teach her. She amused herself by imagining that unwelcome idiot (Donovan, not Greg) as a piece of outdoor furniture, one she would bring to the ground with her mighty arrow.

And then the cleanup: it would probably fall to

her, as all cleanup eventually did. But the tumor of hatred growing inside her would start to dissipate. She would be happy again like she was before her mother died.

There was a knock on her cottage door, and then the doorbell, and then knocking again. "Miss Thompson?"

She recognized the voice as the lawyer who visited weeks ago.

"Please go away," she pled. She stuck her hands, covered in furniture polish, underneath her arm pits.

"Warren Johnson. I need to speak with you about the property. We have to sign some paperwork and... May I come in?"

"No." She slid down the door with her back against it. Ever since her mother died, she had a horrible fear that someone would break down her door and kill her. She'd never seen this monster as an attorney though. "I can't."

"I'm sorry it's taken me so long to get back to you. One of our partners died and the rest of us...well, never mind that. I did deliver the letter as you requested to the Bovant family. I refused to tell them it was you who sent it, as per your wishes."

He cleared his throat and she imagined him loosening his expensive tie.

"If you haven't had a chance to speak with a lawyer, I'll be glad to clear up any questions you have."

"I'll call you when I'm ready. But not now. I'm not signing anything. I can't."

"I'm sure you can appreciate the fact that I drove here especially to see you. I did you the favor of delivering the letter. Might we speak face-to-face?"

"Um...no. I don't think so."

There was hesitancy in her voice, something that made him pause a few minutes longer on her doorstep. He took his monogrammed handkerchief from his pocket and blew his nose with a controlled, steady sound.

"Is it noisy?" Jenna asked.

"Is what noisy?"

"The outside. Everywhere else."

"Outside of town? Um, I don't know what to tell you, Miss Thompson. I suppose it is, yes. Cars and kids and whatnot."

Jenna could hear him shifting on her porch, his body causes creeks and groans on the old wood. He wanted to escape, just like her.

"But certainly something one could adjust to. Have you never been anywhere? Outside of town? I could arrange for you to—"

"Did they hate it that much? That they never want to come back?" Jenna asked.

"Do you mean my clients? They've never discussed that with me specifically, but I can only assume a childhood home is something to outgrow. I'm sure they have fond memories."

"They never lived here. They had cars and expensive stereos and nice rooms. But they never lived here.

It was just their father and hateful stepmother. And of course, all the servants."

"Well then, it's got some sentimental value for you, and probably not so much for them."

Jenna stared at her green couch, cast out from the mansion by the expensive interior decorator when Mrs. Ashton brought over from France. Or maybe it was Italy.

By now, the couch was far from in fashion as it was old and worn, but it was familiar. It suited Jenna more so than the drop-cloth-covered replacement couch in the big house. She didn't belong to the mansion any more than the couch. Bits of hummus fell from her fingers onto the floor and she remembered. Donovan's demise took precedence over everything else.

"Come back in a month, Mr. Johnson. I'll be ready then. I'm in the middle of a project. An important one." Jenna pushed her back against the door and stood, pivoting to face him, or at least the thought of him on the other side of the door.

"If we set up an appointment Miss Thompson, then I won't have to make another unnecessary trip. Does this have something to do with the note I delivered for you? Hello? Miss Thompson, I can help you!"

Jenna was already in the kitchen, plotting her attack.

CHAPTER 21

Donovan

It was almost midnight. Donovan climbed down from the tree, as was his routine, and picked up the many foil packages left for him. They looked like shiny nuggets in the moonlight; each an individual lump of good will from the citizens of Pepperville.

The masking tape labels varied, from simple "left-over roast, ½ baked potato," to personal stories, "you remember last week when I told you I bought new lotion? Well, the dog ate it," to simply, "God Bless you, Donovan." He collected them all, shoving them deep into his pockets. It's hard to say for certain whether he actually read the labels, or just showed his thankfulness by eating what was provided.

Generally, the next thing he did each night was to walk two blocks to Calley's studio. After letting himself in the back door, he went directly to the bathroom to clean up as best he could.

The mirror was off-limits because one evening he

caught sight of himself in Calley's full-length dance mirrors and was shocked by his hollow cheeks and yellow teeth. His coat was now showing signs of wear with a few holes. Most shockingly, his skin had the hardened look of a seasoned, middle-aged farm worker. After three months of tree-living, there was no sign of the clean-cut high school student who once existed in Donovan's body.

On previous occasions, he helped himself to some of Calley's mint magic bars and then removed the latest notes from his pocket left for him by Anessa Jones. His usual routine was to tear the top of the note, the part addressed, "Dear, Dear Donovan," and put the remainder of the heart-covered notebook paper back into his pocket. After turning out the lights, he walked another two blocks to the police station, where he left the notes in the small space between the double glass doors. From there, Donovan headed back to his tree and his life of exile.

The secretary found the notes each morning, and read them with amusement before handing them to a flattered Chief Blank along with his morning coffee. Several times, she suggested that he take the girl out on at least one date. After he did and the notes continued, he realized she was just the type of woman he was looking for. It was obvious Anessa was smitten with him.

CHAPTER 22

Monday

I t was the night of the Pepperville High School musical. Craig Shiardy decided this year he would develop his own script based on the screenplay of his favorite movie, *Gone with the Wind*. He wrote eight musical numbers and hand-picked the lead roles for *Rhett and Scarlett*. He even illustrated a sample program for Emily Wigworth to use when she printed all 146 programs (based on advanced ticket sales) at the *Pepperville Daily Times*.

Craig always wanted to sing on Broadway. As a teenager, his favorite music teacher, Ms. Bogart, told him how gifted he was, and that he really should leave home someday and try to make it big. He had talent. He had style. Craig was going places.

But just like his friends and co-workers, Craig never left Pepperville. He made it to the very edge once, out on Mighton Boulevard to the sign that read, HIGHWAY 32. He glanced at the cars speeding by.

The air smelled sweet like an unfamiliar flower he had neither seen nor smelled before. The grass was taller. The sounds were higher pitched. He didn't understand how seemingly harmless things could feel scary and unfamiliar. Craig turned around and walked home.

Everyone in town knew his voice. When it rained, he opened his second-story apartment window and sang *"Drrrrrop! Splat! Can you hear the rain? Listen close as it flows right down the drain!"*

His rich tenor voice accompanied the booms and blasts of the summer storm to produce a dramatic symphony of rain and voice. Those who were out and about during those rare gifts of precipitation clapped appreciatively.

Craig was determined that even though he'd been too frightened before, his story wouldn't end in Pepperville. Once his project premiered at Pepperville High School he would send his script to bigger venues, and word of his genius would slowly spread until he reached Andrew Lloyd Webber-like proportions. He would become a god among producers when finally his work triumphed on Broadway. News would reach Craig in his living room, where he lounged with sparkling wine while reading entertainment sections of various newspapers heralding his success.

So far, his plan was hitting a few snags.

The Sunday night rehearsal had not gone well. Sharolyn Reekblast, as Scarlett, complained that someone in high school did not need to wear a corset. She wouldn't be able to reach the high notes in the climactic number, *I Know Rhett from Wrong* if she couldn't breathe properly. Craig explained calmly that the corset was essential for the authenticity of the costume and would actually improve her ability to breathe. This fact had recently been confirmed by Calley. (*Secrets to a Scintillating Waist, 1981*)

Craig had been patient with his ingénue for many days now. He relented when Sharolyn refused to smother herself in fake blood during the hospital scene. He even agreed that, as first cousins, Sharolyn and Peter Reekblast should not be sharing an open-mouth kiss as Rhett and Scarlett. But there were things on which he just couldn't compromise.

And so, during dress rehearsal, Sharolyn threw her corset on the stage and stormed out vowing not to return. There were no understudies, as there were barely enough students to round out an entire cast. Craig had no alternative but to send everyone home and remind them to get their beauty rest before the big performance. He assured the rest of the cast that Sharolyn would come to her senses.

She always did.

Craig secretly reveled in his genius. Choosing Sharolyn for the lead had served dual purpose: not only was she beautiful, melodramatic and a perfect size three (the size of the gorgeous costume he found in the community theatre costume closet) she shared a birth date with Vivian Leigh, the original Scarlett O'Hara, causing them to be eternally intertwined in Craig's mind.

As an added bonus, Sharolyn's mother was Winnie Reekblast, rated the number one PR person in the entire state of Iowa by the magazine, "Public Relations Station." Winnie could sell a winter coat to a bear if she so desired.

Winnie tirelessly canvassed neighborhoods, promoting the musical with brochures she designed herself. Each brochure included a detailed biography of both Winnie and Sharolyn, with pictures from their respective days in dance class as well as words of praise from a former voice teacher, a woman who taught both Winnie and her offspring.

For the opening-night performance on Monday, Winnie oversold the auditorium by sixteen, with Craig's consent. They had discussed the possibility of colds and flu resulting in unused chairs.

"It will be a major blow to my cast, Win-Win. They can't look out at the auditorium and see empty seats after months of hard work. No, it simply won't do."

After much negotiation, Winnie agreed. Opening night was typically not as full as the Tuesday matinee, anyway. Die-hard bowlers refused to give up their league spots at the Bowl-Magic, even when Winnie offered to give each bowler $25 and a free bucket of French fries to forego league night. There were only two players interested in the shameless bribe, but they were quickly overruled by their teammates.

The art of bribery required considerably less skill when Winnie approached Miss Yankton's second grade class, where she volunteered every other Thursday.

If they agreed to fill seats on Monday night, she told them, she would personally guarantee an extra chocolate milk for each child during snack time every day the following week. Only one student raised his hand to report a severe allergy to chocolate. He was not given a ticket at the end of class and Winnie made a mental note to call his mother to confirm the information.

The stage was set for the most talked-about affair of the school year. Everyone who was anyone would be in attendance. Craig would later recall the performance—not by the event itself, but by its juxtaposition to other events of that Monday in his self-titled memoir, *Craig*. (We all received one in the mail three Christmases later.) According to Craig, the course of the evening was really determined by a series of unfortunate miscommunications.

As stated in Chapter Seven, *The Wind That Almost Wasn't*, Peter Reekblast confessed to his father that he was experiencing a case of the jitters. His father assured him that those feelings were normal; he, himself, had been a bit nervous before his debut as Tevye in his junior year production of *Fiddler on the Roof*.

His fatherly advice did not end there. Mr. Reekblast promptly headed to the cellar, where last summer's boysenberry wine was reaching its full alcoholic potential. A few nips, he told Peter, would take the edge off the evening's performance.

Had Peter's father first spoken to his wife (the first

miscommunication), he would have discovered that she was making her award-winning *Boysenberry Wine Pork Chops* recipe for dinner. Some of the women competing against her in the county fair thought she won the award strictly because the wine was so strong. "Took the paint right off the Reekblast deck!" according to their next-door neighbor, John Memburly.

The judges passed out soon after sampling the pork chops and could judge no more recipes. This was Peter's favorite dish, and after consuming three or four "nips" with his father, he wolfed down two pork chops and extra sauce. Peter made his stage debut in a state of extreme intoxication.

Craig had begrudgingly asked Anessa and her brother Greg to usher for both performances. Anessa considered it her civic duty to support the high school when asked, since she loved the theatre during her years there. Craig had little faith in their abilities to seat patrons correctly, but no one else would agree to take the position.

The second miscommunication occurred when Anessa allowed the seat-fillers to sit in the empty seats before the lights dimmed, causing havoc when the actual ticket holders arrived right before showtime.

Controversy arose when Winnie unexpectedly— and without an extra ticket— brought her great-aunt, and insisted the elderly woman be seated next to her. Anessa willingly obliged. Winnie always gave Anessa ten dollars if she bagged her groceries.

When the rightful ticketholder arrived, Anessa attempted to seat A-4 in E-14 on the other side of the auditorium, and a second-grader from Miss Yankton's class was forcibly removed from his seat. Tears streamed down the poor child's face, and, just as he was about to throw himself on the floor in complete despair, Winnie tucked a $20 bill in his pocket and explained exactly how much candy that would buy.

The young man skipped happily from the theatre, his teacher following behind him in utter disgust. Only those seated closest to the child observed the harsh dismissal of the hapless grade-schooler, and before they could whisper to those sitting behind them, the lights dimmed.

Craig, who had been peeking out from behind the red velvet curtain, gave an audible sigh of relief. He motioned for Anessa to sit and she willingly obliged as soon as she found Chief Blank seated toward the back of the gym. Greg's attention was harder to acquire, and after several snaps, waves and "pssst," Craig found it necessary to leave his post in order to seat Greg close to the concession stand. That was going to cost Greg at least a dollar when it came time to settle up at the end of the week.

The tape of the Pepperville Marching Band playing *Theme from Rhett and Scarlett by Craig Shiardy* (as duly noted in the program) echoed across the crowded gymnasium. There was no way to include the band in the live performance, since every available warm body was needed for the stage crew. In addition to that, every single folding chair in Pepperville was in use.

Another of Craig's ingenious ideas was to rig the tape recorder so that it played over the sound system; the sophomore electronics class, as per Craig's instructions, also re-worked the tape recorder so that it was run entirely by remote control. Craig had previously seen disastrous results from a careless actor bumping the tape recorder to the "on" position while exiting the stage. He figured that with the sound completely under his control, music mishaps could be avoided.

Even though his masterpiece was about to begin, Craig couldn't take his eyes off Anessa and Chief Blank. They were such an odd, and also fitting, couple; this silly, empty-headed store clerk and a serious, yet in some ways, equally empty-headed policeman.

Anessa snuggled her head into the shoulder of the police chief. He in turn placed a muscular arm around his girlfriend. Her thick, fuchsia sweater left substantial fuzz on the floor underneath her seat. Craig noticed (as did several others, who later discussed it with righteous indignity over coffee and donuts) that Chief Blank's head was coated with the same bits of pink fuzzy material.

The curtain parted. The audience gave an audible gasp when they viewed the elaborate set depicting Scarlett's plantation home, Tara. Craig and some of the art students spent two months detailing the tree-lined drive with thousands of green- and gold-painted leaves. Tara itself was a white-and-gold, sheet-rock masterpiece. Thirteen pounds of gold glitter had been donated by Ted's Crematorium to adorn the columns on either side of the centerpiece: a monstrously huge, white door.

Detailed scenes depicting every day plantation life, slave cabins, and Southern belles adorned the doorway. A faux-brass knocker, composed entirely of papier-mâché, was molded into the shape of Sharolyn's head and painted with the same shade of lustrous gold as the leaves.

When Sharolyn entered from stage left on cue (as Craig had no doubt she would), there were more "ooohs" and "aaahs." She possessed Barbie-doll perfection, complete with deep, blue eyes and a small, turned-up nose. The tightened corset accentuated her already perfect figure.

Her magnificent blond hair had been sprayed with something resembling a shellac finish. The glare off the up-do gave a few audience members strong headaches, they would later report. Craig refused to let her wear a wig, nor did he want her to dye her locks. In his mind, Scarlett was eternally blond.

As the show progressed, there were a couple of small goofs: one chorus member sang the wrong song for his solo, and another inserted a burp at a most inopportune moment. The worst gaffe came when a stage hand became overzealous with the fake blood, and the somber hospital scene turned into something of an ice-skating party.

Peter had forgotten a few lines but for the most

part, was right on target. His alcohol consumption had done just what his father had predicted—it loosened him up to provide for an enjoyable stage experience.

The climactic number, *I Know Rhett from Wrong*, involved Sharolyn singing solo for the first stanza and Peter joining her on stage for the second and third. The duet was quite moving, bringing every member of the Reekblast family to tears. Even her Uncle Marvin, who was running the video camera, sobbed noticeably. He was always chosen to record performances for his heretofore steady hand and lack of emotion. Craig, too, enjoyed the moment. Everything was going just as Craig planned.

When the two finished the song, Sharolyn leaned in for the scripted kiss. Peter, now entrenched fully in the character of Rhett and still considerably inebriated, opened his mouth and quite visibly stuck his tongue into the unsuspecting mouth of his first cousin.

Sharolyn's eyes widened with surprise. Peter held tightly to the back of her head making her extraction, had she tried, impossible. Sharolyn though, was the consummate actress and refused to break character. Peter released her head and retracted the offending tongue after several painfully silent seconds.

Peter's father struggled to move from his seat and finally gave up. The after-effects of too many pork chops overrode his need to cover the eyes of his ashen-faced wife. Craig was fortunate enough to catch Winnie's eye. He motioned for her to clap and she did so, jumping to her feet and applauding with a vigor normally reserved for Calley Sthenics.

The rest of the audience sat motionless, horrified by what had just taken place.

Were it any other night, such an awkward display of genetic affiliation would have been the dominant source of gossip for the next several months. (And indeed, it did pop up in conversation some years later, when Peter blamed his thirst for lacy underthings on an unfortunate event at his high school play.) Under normal circumstances, it would have been the talk of the town for weeks. But this evening would be remembered as anything but normal.

Craig turned to the actors and crew behind him. He clapped vigorously, encouraging them to do the same. Most had not seen what had taken place on stage but did as instructed. "You see!" Craig whispered. "Some understand the true sacrifice an actor must make for their craft!" The next few minutes of the performance passed without incident.

The cast was preparing for the final number, which involved all of the actors as well as the chorus and the prop and make-up crews. Every single voice was needed to make this the showstopper it was intended to be.

Craig had only rehearsed with the full cast twice, because there were so many conflicts of activities within the high school. In full costume, the area back-stage became complete chaos as all scrambled for the stage.

The audience didn't seem to notice what happened next, as the buzz surrounding *The Kiss* had reached a fevered pitch. This was the point of the third, and most dramatic, miscommunication of the evening: Winnie Reekblast had failed to notify Craig that she had oversold the auditorium by thirty-five, not sixteen.

Why was this important? Because the overflow crowd had to stand in the back of the gym without the benefit of a folding chair on which to rest. Some of the weary souls leaned against the rolled-up wrestling mats stored next to the concession stand.

Brad and Ruby (the couple whose romance led to the demise of her sister, Rosie) bought eight overflow tickets, one for each of them and their six children. At the last minute, Ruby announced she would not be attending due to a spectacular headache that was the result of ongoing conflict with her husband and a day of unruly children.

Brad reluctantly brought the children alone, but the first soliloquy by Peter proved entirely too long for his short attention span. His children, ranging in age from eight to three, were listening intently from their perches atop the wrestling mats. As he decided to slip out for a quick beer at the Bowl-Mor, he leaned down and whispered in the ear of his tow-headed five-year-old.

Craig watched him walk out and felt extremely agitated over the notion that someone would simply abandon *his* directorial debut, and also that these children, known to all the town for their unruly behavior, were left unattended.

He tried unsuccessfully to get the attention of Anessa, who seemed more interested in rubbing the thigh of her new boyfriend. The sign language he used with Winnie wasn't working either. Greg Prembone had fallen asleep against the back wall, his mouth hanging open with a thick stream of drool washing over his jaw.

Craig made a mental note to dock him another dollar.

Brad's precocious five-year-old didn't waste time after his father left. After several minutes of poking his siblings, those in the back row turned and shushed him sternly. Eventually, he wandered away and walked along the perimeter of the gym. He was fascinated by *The Kiss* and paused briefly to absorb the sight of his babysitter embracing someone older than his brothers and sisters.

When it was over, he continued his journey—behind the basketball hoops and finally to the backstage area—remaining completely unnoticed.

While Craig fluffed the skirts of several extras, the remote control to the sound system sat in a state of vulnerability on Craig's stool. The little boy picked up this new toy and walked away, coolly and unconcerned, back to the rear of the gymnasium where his siblings had also become restless.

The big, blue rubber mat, used for the Pepperville wrestling team's workouts, was rolled up and lying horizontally in the corner. It was a new piece of equipment in the indoor playground created just this evening. It was proving just too tempting for Brad and Ruby's children.

All of them, including the five year old carrying his new prize, jumped, rolled or bounced on the mat like they were on a trampoline. Why they had never discovered this playground before was beyond them. The little boy got on his stomach and wiggled behind the mat, where he began to experiment with the buttons on this new device.

The large cast assembled onstage and Craig prepared to direct the final number. He hadn't yet noticed the remote control was missing, but the abrupt sound of the band filled the air before he could think. It rose quickly, until it was so loud Winnie's great-aunt had to remove both of her hearing aids.

Craig looked around in dismay, quickly realizing his remote control was no longer where he left it. He immediately thought of the art department, a bunch of pranksters who initially painted bathroom humor about Scarlett on the unfinished Tara set. There were others within the school system who might want to exact some kind of revenge on him for one perceived slight or another, but now wasn't the time to speculate. Something had to be done and done quickly, since the audience was starting to panic.

In the beginning of Chapter Eight, *What We Do for Our Craft,* Craig explains his internal struggle that night:

I didn't want to shut down the musical, my baby, in its debut performance. An audience truly well-versed in theatre performance would have stuck it out, no matter the damage to their ear drums, but this was Pepperville.

I couldn't see the dark backstage area well enough to search for the lost remote control. The cast stood at attention, still wearing the expressions of their individual characters just as I'd taught them. Even the hair and makeup cast members knew their place.

At that point, I did the only thing I could. Sure, I could go back and think of a million different options, but that doesn't change that night.

Craig quickly made his way behind the worn, red-velvet curtain and down the backstage steps to an alcove next to the gym door. He opened the power box and threw the main circuit breaker, plunging the auditorium into quiet darkness. He let out a loud sigh. It was like he had just sacrificed a child. *His* child.

As soon as the gymnasium went dark, the crowd became silent. The children who become restless and fussy stared ahead in amazement. Craig hesitated for just a moment, trying to decide how he would direct the cast if they could not see his hands. A few people tried in vain to navigate the rows of knees and dress-up shoes to make their exit. When they realized it was impossible to leave such a crowded room without a light of some kind, a sense of resignation settled in and they returned to their seats.

At this point, Craig thought about giving the audience their money back and scheduling another performance for Saturday. A musical without a big finish wasn't a musical at all. He even considered serving a buffet of cold roast beef and cheese to thank the audience members for coming back.

If his cast wasn't able to sing the final number, it would fall to him.

His sweet tenor voice filled the air, almost operatic in its vibrato and perfect pitch. Soon Winnie joined in, harmonizing and adding her own words to *Send Him North*. The faceless cast joined in as they stood, arms intertwined at the waist in a show of solidarity. When the entire group finished, all at slightly different intervals due to the fact that Craig was unable to cut them off visually as a director, the crowd applauded enthusiastically.

A few brave parents fumbled to the stage with flowers specially packaged for the performance from Flowers, Flowers and Fudge. Chief Blank took his official, miniature patrol flashlight from his back pocket and escorted people to the exits.

The evening, despite a disastrous turn of events, had actually turned out to be a huge success.

CHAPTER 23

Jenna

We all agreed that the events that transpired that evening were either the result of a weather phenomenon or a hex placed by a passengers overhead in a passing plane.

Main Street was completely desolate. The high school musical, the biggest social event of the season left Jenna with convenient opening to pull off her biggest trick yet.

Squish.Squish. Squish.

Her red boots sounded especially loud tonight because the street was vacant, and there was only the slightest hint of wind to carry the sound ahead of her. The echo reminded her of the Ashton ballroom. She and her mother used to call back and forth to each other, giggling as their voices reverberated throughout the cavernous space.

When she left her cottage approximately fifteen minutes earlier, her goal had been to destroy Donovan.

For whatever reason, with each step her resolve weakened. The birth-control-laden hummus, tucked under the arm of her wool coat, felt cool against her side.

Her mother wouldn't have understood. She would have ignored Donovan until such a time as he died of old age, and he and the branches he sat on came crashing to the ground.

She would have smiled the half-aware smile she used when conversing with her daughter. Vivienne would have turned away as Jenna explained the whole sordid story. That someone with evil motives had just splattered all over Main Street, taking the branches of the oldest, most beautiful tree in town to the ground with him.

As she confided in me later, she had a sudden moment of clarity: *Maybe Donovan felt the same powerlessness. Maybe when the other wrestler died, he felt like it was his fault. Maybe his "loving" family forced him to become a person he simply wasn't. Maybe no one listened to him, either. Maybe he was trapped.*

She continued on, trying to absorb this revelation. Could it be the power he had over the people of her town was really no power at all? Was he unable to understand how the rest of his world, full of red-heads and empty boasts continued to function despite his grief?

She stopped when the next revelation hit like a tornadic gust of wind:

Was her mother—the woman who controlled the

Ashton staff, and at one time managed the huge, empty property—just as trapped by her own life?

She had no friends, no family, no world outside the one framed by the mansion gates.

Beyond rare trips to the doctor and school activities, Jenna never witnessed her mother interacting with the rest of Pepperville. Had Jenna been wrong in assuming all along that her mother wanted creature comforts? Had she wanted more than expensive jewelry and the acquisition of the property around her, as Jenna had imagined? Did her mother simply desire a life beyond her self-imposed prison?

Squishsquishsquish.

She walked quicker with each memory of her mother's death. They were coming fast and hard, washing over her like high tide, and she was unable to breathe under all of the water.

Despite the speed at which she walked, she wasn't able to escape them. There she was, mindlessly going about her adulthood in much the same manner her mother had. She was continuing the family legacy of routine and seclusion, and she cringed at the thought that she hated a poor, frustrated young man for doing the exact same thing.

As soon as she reached Donovan's tree, she realized he was awake and seemingly alert; not at all like he was during the day. She was forming the words in her head but still not believing them possible. Jenna looked up at him, sitting as he always did with his arms draped around his knees.

"I've hated you since the day you arrived," she announced. "You came into our town and disrupted our perfect rhythm." She squinted into the near darkness that wasn't quite lighted by a nearby street lamp.

"I saw you on television at the State Wrestling Championship. I saw your eyes... That picture hasn't left my head once. All of this time, I had convinced myself it was arrogance. But you were—are—so...*lonely*."

Now that she'd dare utter those words out loud, the rest tumbled out easily.

"You had such a big family and all sorts of people around you, and you were still lonely," she continued. "That's what really made me mad when you showed up in the tree. What right did you have to be here? You haven't had to make it on your own." Jenna paused.

She noticed the big welts on the sides of Donovan's face. There was still blood on his knuckles and around some of his fingernails. Another bratty kid throwing things at him, she thought.

"I heard about that boy who died, and it took me a while, but I think I get it. I understand why you hate yourself."

She wanted desperately to connect with him, to see his eyes. "You think you were responsible for his happiness, even though you haven't done so well with your own. We've both made things unnecessarily difficult for ourselves, it would seem." She had to sit down. It had taken a man up a tree and a murderous plot to regain her sanity.

"Jenna? Your mother has cancer. She has for quite some time."

Doctor Frantz's face was pale and rigid. He spoke slowly and matter-of-factly like he was giving directions to the county fair. "I told her several years ago that she needed to go to Stanswick and begin an aggressive treatment regimen. She said she didn't have the money. As her long-time physician, I felt I needed to do what I could to help your mother. Last month I talked to Drake Ashton about covering the expenses, and he declined." His lips tightened and he set his clipboard carefully on his knee. *"There isn't much to be done at this point. I know you're young and this is a heavy burden. But I also know what a strong young lady you are. You'll get through this and someday, the sun will be shining and you'll look up and realize life is good again."*

The funeral was elaborate; the coffin was light pink with gold, swirling trim. Fenderson said he had received the largest flower order ever, courtesy of Drake Ashton's attorney. Exotic multi-colored blooms draped every inch of the coffin. A large wreath read, "Loving Mother" and an Ashton cousin she'd never seen before, stood at the podium, thanking Jenna and her mother for years of dedicated service.

Jenna was inconsolable. Somewhere in the

weeping and moaning and aching over her loss, a former maid, eight months pregnant and not about to mince words, whispered in her ear that Jenna was an Ashton who should now make her claim on the estate.

Mr. Ashton slept with all of the help, from laundry mistress to un-utilized nannies, the voice had said. The entire staff knew that Jenna was the unfortunate product of her mother's employment.

Another maid overhearing the conversation said, "there's no one left to care for you, so you'll need to protect yourself."

Her mother had been sleeping with the late Mr. Ashton, out of duty or love, no one would ever know. But Jenna was the end result. Her mother's punishment didn't end with the birth of her bastard child. Nineteen years later she would writhe in agony, destroyed from the inside out because her daughter's family refused to pay for her treatment. Now Jenna was alone, and the burden only hers to carry on.

The hummus dip she had so carefully prepared hit the ground with a thump and the plastic lid opened slightly, emptying half of the hormonally-charged contents into the root system of the magnificent maple.

She was the common denominator. Donovan's

prison; her mother's prison; a future as a maid living in a big house, it made sense.

Jenna had to find the strength to move on. It's exactly what her mother would want for her. There was no turning back.

"Do you want to get out of here? With me?"

Donovan looked down at her. For the first time in his self-imposed exile, he gazed without hesitation into the eyes of another human being. There was a cut over one brow, now caked with blood that increased the intensity of his gaze.

His dirty, blond hair hung limply around his face. He pulled his bony fingers from one pocket and squeezed his grimy hand into a fist. It was thin and frail, unlike the muscular capable hands that first climbed the tree three months earlier. He opened his mouth to speak and then closed it again. Once more he tried, and this time, actual words came out.

"Yes. I want to leave," he said quietly. It was a surprisingly simple exchange that brought an end to the most bizarre public spectacle in Pepperville's lengthy history of oddities.

Written on several postcards sent to Anessa six months later and posted on the corkboard at the front of the Shoppe and Walke, Jenna noted Donovan's agility over the next few minutes. Someone who had spent months sitting in one position maneuvered himself nimbly from one branch to the next and lowered himself to the ground without incident. He had no luggage, no special mementos, nothing to remind him that for one small moment in time he lived in a tree in the middle of Pepperville.

The other side of the postcards, incidentally, were pictures from Wyoming, Idaho, and Washington. Across the bottom of the last postcard, trees carpeted the landscape in the deep, well-nourished green of early spring. Above the landscape was wide, blue sky; endless, without borders.

CHAPTER 24

Pepperville

"The events of Monday night were quickly overshadowed by the actions of one Miss Jenna Thompson," read the lengthy headline on Wednesday's last page of the *Pepperville Daily Times*. Page three included a story on the forced power outage during the musical, and a picture of Chief Blank in a reenactment the next day with his miniature flashlight. The caption underneath read: "Chief Blank Lights Our Way."

While the rest of the town enjoyed the talents of the Reekblast family, Jenna and Donovan walked to her home through empty streets. Neither said a word until they were safely behind closed doors.

Jenna gave him a towel and soap so that Donovan could shower for the first time in months. The clothes she offered him had been sitting in the work room of Ashton Mansion for years, probably left by some hapless gardener who was fired during a drunken rage by Mrs. Ashton and never allowed to pick up his things. At least they were clean.

Jenna tended to Donovan's wounds and cut his hair, although he hadn't asked her to do so. The more she did to help him, the quicker her feelings of hatred dissolved.

The conversation between them was stilted; she asked stupid questions and he answered with one word or two. But neither of them were big conversationalists when they were feeling on top of the world. This was, at least, a start.

She packed everything she owned in the suitcase the doctor had given her mother when he encouraged her to seek treatment in Stanswick. She took the keys to the Pontiac that Drake Ashton had so prized during his short summer visits, and then made one final sweep of her cottage. All of the money she had saved from cleaning both for Calley and the Ashton's—$38,500— fit neatly in a shoebox.

They pulled out of the long Ashton driveway, Donovan carefully balancing Jenna's fishbowl on his lap. Jenna drove down Main Street, and across Mighton Boulevard, and then Willowood. The sign in front of them read: HIGHWAY 32, with an arrow pointing left, and another below: STANSWICK 67 with an arrow pointing to the right.

Jenna sighed and glanced at Donovan, trying to ignore the quickly-developing gurgle in her stomach. He nodded solemnly. For the first time in several months, the corners of his mouth turned slightly upward. She pressed the left turn signal. The tires slowly rolled on the pristine pavement, something that should have been documented at that moment for its rarity.

Someone had really left Pepperville; someone born and raised there, with no outside connections. *The Something* that happened—more than the musical, more than Donovan coming down from the tree—was Jenna Thompson finally coming into her own.

Last year, I received a festive, pre-printed Christmas card that read, "Merry Christmas! Love, Donovan, Jenna, and Sunshine." Inside was a handwritten note, not the form letters I have so detested through the years. There was also a picture of a smiling, blonde girl in a lacrosse uniform. On the back, scrawled in a child's handwriting: *Sunshine Bovant, age 8.*

I placed the letter in a drawer and refrained from reading it until leaves started peeking out on the trees. It was painful to remember Pepperville as it once was, with predictable Jenna, Fenderson's Fudge and all of the other familiar faces.

The guilt had been eating away at me for over ten years. It's not like I was the first, and certainly wasn't the last. But the town and everyone in it was a part of me, and it felt as though I had chewed off my own leg.

The population of my hometown briefly dwindled

and the remaining residents, desperate to hang on to their homes and way of life sent out letters begging for help revitalizing the town. I turned my back. I did this in much the same manner I had turned my back on Jenna when she was so alone and needing anyone to guide her.

No thanks to me, these days the *Welcome to Pepperville* sign is sporting a fresh coat of paint and new homes have sprouted up on along Highway 32. There is renewed vigor, though little exists to mark the fact that we all lived through those strange times.

I don't believe Jenna understood what she set in the day of the State Wrestling Championship. The whole world turned upside down, and Jenna and Donovan just left it all behind without as much as a nod goodbye.

I have to believe poor Donovan would have stayed up in that tree for years without her intervention. Maybe not so good for Donovan, but Old Pepperville would still be in existence. Once those two left, it was like a pinhole had was created in the damn. People started leaking out a few at a time until the personality that was once my hometown existed no more.

Fenderson Reekblast ran off with his sister-in-law for parts unknown. Sharolyn was never the same and left some years later with a passing trucker. I heard a rumor she owns a real estate business now, but dabbled in "Avant-garde films," whatever that might be. Maybe a waste of theatrical talent, depending on how you look at it.

And speaking of theatre, Craig Shiardy decided to write about that Monday and how it changed his hometown. After years of contacting publishers, one finally showed some interest in The Something That Happened in Pepperville. Craig demanded a ride in a black limousine with tinted windows to a book signing as a part of his book deal.

The publisher obliged and after a slow ride up and down Main Street (and past his mother's home) he hired the limo to take him all the way to New York City. That was the last we saw of Craig. I heard a rumor that he used the money to produce his musical somewhere down south.

Many people I've spoken with feel resentment towards Jenna. They didn't have the courage—or the knowledge—or whatever it took to get out of town on their own, and they certainly didn't know how to get rid of Donovan. But little-ol', grumpy Jenna did.

Jenna never returned to Pepperville. Neither did Donovan, so I have to wonder if they did feel a little guilty. But then again, neither of them had a reason to return to a town that, to them, only represented pain.

It's unfortunate that the demise of the Old Pepperville always seems to rest on the tiny shoulders of, then nineteen-year-old, Jenna. Those I've kept in contact with always mention her name as if it were a bitter fruit incapable of being digested. I've never disagreed with them, I'm ashamed to admit. But how could I fault her for feeling just as I did: that there must be more to life? The Pepperville that people thought existed, the one that seemed like its own snow globe, was dead. There were some who just couldn't (or wouldn't) accept it. Some folks just don't like change.

Don't get me wrong; this wasn't the end of a little town; it was actually somewhat of a rebirth. When someone finally steps into the water and proves to everyone else that its only ankle deep, it becomes one giant pool party. That's what our Jenna did, she stepped into the water.

At first people just trickled out a few at a time, and always at night. It was something they must have felt was wrong. They would return with trinkets from the outside world to show their family when they were sure no one was watching. The whole world was like a shiny new penny and each trip brought more incredible stories and new and wondrous objects.

Eventually, it became commonplace to travel. People came and went; came and went until both sides of the highway needed repaving. They visited relatives in Stanswick and all of the little towns nearby. Families gathered in homes previously only viewed in pictures.

There were vacation pictures from beaches and hills. I even heard last year of one couple driving all the way to Massachusetts; several *days* drive. Amazing! It was as if our little town was finally a part of the world.

There were big changes in town as well. Flowers, Flowers and Fudge began carrying candies from exotic places like Georgia and South Dakota. Callie started taking classes in all the new aerobics dance moves and opened up another studio in Stanswick. One of those Bovant girls—I can't keep them straight—works as her assistant. Postmistress Charlotte O'Cann even tried making a trip in the daylight. Unfortunately, she got a flat tire and took that as a bad omen. Far as I know, she never left again. The mailboxes are still filled with letters and bills in the middle of the night.

When the toothpaste factory opened on the edge of town, there was a real need for housing. "Pepper Heights," they call it. It's quite a fancy place. I've heard they have a nine-hole golf course and a fountain; and someday, a statue. Residents ride their bikes to the Shoppe and Walke, a trendy little health-food store, but not because there isn't a road. They linger for coffee and pastries while reading the Pepperville Daily Times, still printed thrice weekly. The town has now come full circle: Instead of people clamoring to leave, folks are actually moving to Pepperville.

My time to leave came a few years back. I looked out my door and didn't recognize anyone walking down the street. It was time to go. As much as I thought about it, even I had never gone anywhere. Old habits die hard, you know.

One day, I licked my finger, stuck it in the air and waited for the feel of the wind. Things just seemed right. I packed up that day. I couldn't resist the call to warmth and greenery; more importantly, things in Pepperville had just changed too much for my taste.

I dated a woman very seriously for a year or two. I told her I came from Iowa but didn't elaborate.

Pepperville was a secret I had hidden so well that I almost convinced myself it had never existed.

Now here's where I have to let you in on my secret, because as I told you earlier, everyone in Pepperville had one. Mine isn't so big, unless you decide there are further implications, but I personally can't think too hard about it. You'll understand.

My mother also worked at Ashton Mansion. She was the head cook until shortly before my birth. On her death bed, my Dear Wife confessed to me that in her administrative job at the hospital, she uncovered my true date of birth. It wasn't the birthdate I'd celebrated my entire life, but some four months earlier than I'd always been led to believe.

My mother had been nine months pregnant when she quit working for the Ashton estate, and only married my father after I had entered the world. She was a victim of Old Man Ashton, just as Jenna's mother had been.

Here's one more, now that I'm spilling them. I purchased Ashton Mansion, under the condition that Jenna was told it was Drake himself offering the sale. It seemed like the right thing to do for a sister I had never acknowledged. Since we never had children, My Dear Wife and I, there was quite a savings account just sitting there with no real purpose.

I approached the boys as discreetly as possible after Jenna's mother passed. I wanted Jenna to think that the Ashton family had actually turned over a new leaf and had done something nice for her.

Guess the guilt had gotten to me at that point, and I felt like I had to do something to ensure she had a permanent residence. I know: too little too late, right? It was quite a challenge to meet with their attorney privately. Few things were really under the radar in Pepperville in those days.

The boys didn't want to sell at first; and after I signed the papers, I paid the attorney a few hundred extra so that the Ashtons wouldn't find out I was going to turn around and sell it again—to the maid.

Doubt they would have agreed, had they known. Wouldn't have looked good for them to be treating the help as an equal in a real estate transaction. It was a sweetheart deal I was offering her. It really was. Too bad she didn't go for it. I guess she had bigger plans.

Anyway, the property became too much for me and I sold it to a big-time movie producer. He saw it while driving through on his way to a luxury home up north. He was really taken by the old place and promised to keep it painted and mowed and looking like it hadn't in many years. Last I heard, they were planning to make some teen horror movie there.

In any case, it would be used and well-kept and I felt that I had, in some small way, done my part to preserve the quirky little town I once called home.

Finally, one snowy February morning, I opened the drawer and removed the note, written on green Christmas stationery. It was written in gold, glittery ink; so festive and happy, so unlike Jenna:

Dear Friend,

I know this is a surprise, but I found your address while I was at work. Things are wonderful here in rainy Seattle. I have been working for the public library for almost three years. Donovan gave up his position as an accountant last year to devote more time to his wood-working business and be a stay-at-home dad. He has crafted the most beautiful wooden horses for all of the neighborhood children, and his "hobby" has become quite the business venture.

Sunshine is the delight of our world. She possesses a never-ending exuberance for life about her that neither Donovan, nor I ever mastered. The girl has never met a stranger.

It's somewhat ironic that Donovan, who struggles to communicate with everyone, learned to sign before I did. But it hasn't slowed down our girl one bit. She loves to dance and just recently won first place in her all-school speech contest. She has even taught her father to sign a few curse words.

Every year for her birthday she asks only for one thing, and Donovan and I have decided it's time to oblige. We have never thought it was important to have a marriage license, but our daughter disagrees. Sunshine would like us to have a formal wedding ceremony in our back yard. It is important to her that we hang a wedding portrait on our wall and "quit embarrassing her." She insists on cake and punch and lots of people. All of the things we try and avoid. But we'll do it for her. We plan to make it official in late January with a few close friends.

Hope all is well with you.
Happy Holidays!
Jenna, Donovan and Sunshine

P.S. I received a card from Anessa and Sean the other day. They just had their fifth child!

Anessa still works at the lingerie store and Sean has been promoted to head traffic cop (is that what they're called?) for the city of Des Moines.

I had another dream. I was walking down a quiet street in a suburb, clothed in my summer pajamas and brown suede slippers, on a street lined with lollipop-shaped trees and decorated on each porch with barrels bursting with brightly-colored flowers. I was drawn to one particular house similar to my childhood home across the alley from Ashton Mansion. It was perfectly manicured and new and unlike anything I had experienced in my childhood and yet completely familiar. A friendly Cocker Spaniel jumped off the porch swing to greet me.

I paused to pet him briefly, and then grasped the shiny, metal knob. I was hesitant to enter, given my previous dream experiences, so I opened the door only a crack. I heard birds chirping and felt the whisper of a soft breeze against my face. I threw the door open wide to expose a vast, gently rolling space. Though I could still hear birds, none were visible; only a deep green carpet of grass as far as the eye could see. The slight breeze carried a scent I remembered well: that of my dear wife's perfume. I breathed in deeply and exhaled. The grass looked so appealing, I lay down; the soft blades gently caressed me with each new wave of air. I could feel my entire body relaxing, one achy muscle at a time.

Finally, I would sleep.

BONUS Story

Act One

Craiglund Charles Shiardy had always been a theatre standout. He'd won a HISSI award (High School Standout Ingenue) as a freshman, a task unheard of prior to his arrival. His sophomore year, he was cast as

Cletus, the lead in *Chillin' in Chatsworth*. Junior year, Craig and Betsy Truman shared the stage as they portrayed Patricia and Richard Nixon in *Water Under the Gate: A Musical*. Everything was going his way until the spring musical, when Ms. Bogart, the theatre teacher caught mono.

Right in the middle of month two of rehearsals for *Bungled; The Untrue Story of Abraham Lincoln*, she called in sick and never returned. Ms. Bogart had always pulled Craig aside when she was going to be away. "Now, Craig, there's no need for you to come to rehearsal tomorrow. I've got a dental appointment and the kids will just torture you. No real rehearsal happening anyway. "No one else in his life had ever supported him the way she did.

The production fell into the hands of assistant director and retired mortician, Ruth Minch. Ruth had been a star thespian in high school, though much about theatre had changed since her day. For starters, they had three microphones stands in front of the stage now. Ruth insisted the actors yell as loud as possible, unwilling to accept this new development.

From the very start, Ruth didn't understand nor appreciate Craig's unique style. As he was reciting the key soliloquy, Abraham Lincoln's diatribe about the theater and how he secretly hated it, she walked out on stage. Every kid, no matter how long they'd been in theatre, knew you didn't walk onstage without warning.

Instead of giving verbal instructions, Ruth Minch

grabbed Craig on either side of his face and turned his head away from the portrait of George Washington and toward the audience. She pivoted and left the stage without comment.

When Craig, mouth agape, stood in silence, she commanded, "finish your lines, young man!"

That was the day Craig did the one thing he promised himself he would never do: he walked out.

In his favorite teacher's absence, he'd been taunted in every way. The simple-minded, "theater class is an easy A," group snickered at his self-made purple sparkly slippers, the ones he'd spent hours sewing the sequins on.

The girls who were secretly jealous of his fashion sense waited for him after school. They followed him home, chanting all the way, "Craig wears his mother's clothes. Craig plays with dolls. Craig eats crumpets."

Then there was the time he was eating his lunch and the extras walked by his table, dumping their ketchup-filled tray into his lap. They giggled and kept walking.

He had no idea this resentment had been bubbling up for years. Other hopeful actors had been unhappy by Craig's constant lead performer status and until Ms. Bogart's absence, were afraid to tell him so. Now they walked away when he began to speak and snickered behind his back.

He was truly alone.

As he'd left the stage, he heard another actor mutter, "good riddance." That was the thing that got him right in the gut. He'd always tried his best to befriend everyone—from stage hands to lighting, chorus to understudy, he was never too big to say hello. That was how the real theatre folk, the ones who became legends, behaved.

Tonight, as he rode his bike away from Pepperville High School, he cursed the tears forming in his eyes. Craiglund was so much stronger than this. He'd gone onstage the last night of his performance freshman year with strep throat and a fever of 101 degrees. It would take more than this to break him.

He reached the corner of Plum and Second, where he would normally turn left on Plum to go home. Instead, he turned right. Many nights he'd parked his bike in front of Ms. Bogart's apartment building, trying to find the courage to go knock on her door. He wasn't in love with her, but he knew a kindred spirit when he saw one. He'd watched as she danced in front of her window to a mysterious piece he assumed was theatrical in nature. She was mesmerizing.

He only had to knock once before she threw the door open. The smell of menthol rub and cinnamon wafted into the hallway, causing his eyes to water. *Good. She wouldn't suspect he'd been crying.* Ms. Bogart's normally impeccably coiffed copper hair was hanging in odd clumps around her head. Her bright and shiny eyes were watery and bleary.

"Ms. Bogart? I'm sorry to bother you. I know you're under the weather, but I...just quit the production. I couldn't do it, not without you there."

Now that he had a moment to study her, he worried that she might be drunk. She had the same tell-tale off-balance stance and unfocused eyes his stepfather did after a night at the bar. "I'm sorry. This was a mistake. I should go."

"No, wait!" she grabbed his arm, her chipped red nails digging into his skin. "I've missed you, Craig. Please stay."

She moved aside and allowed him to enter her small apartment, where posters from the biggest theatrical productions of the last three decades adorned her walls. Craig glanced around as if he'd entered a museum. "This is...it's wonderful, Ms. Bogart. Did you see all of these?"

"I'm not that brave. My cousin did. He sent me every single poster. You'll notice this one is signed by Clark Gable."

Craig bent down and squinted. "'Thank you for a wonderful evening. All my deepest devotion, Clark.' Ms. Bogart, did your cousin—"

"I don't ask questions, Craig, and neither should you. "She coughed hard into a tissue in her hands.

Now he realized it was illness, not alcohol causing her symptoms and he felt relief. He felt guilty for doubting the most brilliant woman he'd ever met.

"Despite how I sound, I'm doing much better. Sit down and tell me what's going on with you. It has to be serious for you to stop by my place like this."

She motioned toward a brown plush couch.

It reminded Craig of the Truth Chair he'd sat on

during the one-act, from *All Honesty* because the minute his rear hit the cushion, he began telling her about his miserable life. He didn't stop until she was updated on every minute detail.

"No one likes me. I see that now. I don't know where I go from here. Theatre is my life. It's in my blood. "He reached down and grabbed a tissue for himself from a mountain of them sitting on her coffee table.

Ms. Bogart leaned forward and patted his leg. "Oh dear. I was worried that might happen when I left. You're different than everyone else, Craig. I'm sure you've figured that out by now. People in Pepperville don't appreciate folks who follow their own rules. You may even leave town someday, who knows."

He blew his nose and nodded. "Thank you for saying that, Ms. Bogart. It doesn't help me right now, though. I've got two more weeks of junior year and then the entirety of my senior year to get through first."

"Craig, you couldn't have come on a better night. Before you came to my door, I had a call from an old friend. He wants me to take on a project at the community college this summer. You can't take the theatre out of the theatrical for long, can you?"

"You're right about that, Ms. Bogart. "He smiled enthusiastically, pleased to have someone in his corner once again.

"They want me to direct this summer's performance. We're doing *Row Your Way to Happiness*. Have you heard of it? It's a musical about three friends who–"

"Spend a month in a boat, lost at sea. They compose an entire musical, which becomes a huge hit on Broadway. I know them all."

"I forgot that wonderful trait of yours, Craig. "She smiled in appreciation of him. "When I read the script, I thought, you know who would make the perfect Tony? My Craig, that's who."

Craig blushed. He'd not expected this incredible turn of events. "But don't you have to audition everyone for the role?"

She pushed the air away with her hand. "Just a formality. You're my Tony. I do need to warn you though, these are college students. They may be even more challenging than your high school friends. I have less control over these folks."

Act Two

After the audition process, Craig waited by the phone for two anxious days. It wasn't that he didn't trust Ms. Bogart's words, it was more that he didn't trust his talent.

While watching auditions, he'd realized his placement as lead in every high school musical had been at her behest and maybe not because he was any better than the others trying out. There was real talent at Pepperville Community College.

"Hello Tony, "she sang to the tune of *Rowing on a Monday,* when he picked up the phone halfway through the first ring.

"Did I get it?"

"Don't be coy, Craig. You know that doesn't work with me. I'll expect you in the theatre at seven sharp on Monday?"

"Got it. Seven p.m."

Ms. Bogart cleared her throat. "I must've forgotten

to mention that we will have rehearsals twice daily for the foreseeable future. Our mornings will begin with stretches and a little bit of dancing, followed by line rehearsals. You'll return at four p.m. for intense acting lessons. You're not in high school anymore, Craig. This is the big time."

While he'd dreamed of this day forever, it gave him pause thinking his entire summer would be consumed by his role as Tony in *Row Your Way to Happiness*.

"Yes, I'll be there. Oh, and Ms. Bogart? Is there something I should do? You know, to make sure the other students like me? They may be offended that someone younger got a lead."

Ms. Bogart laughed her laugh that made Craig think of the bells he heard at the church Christmas celebration. He'd missed that sound.

"You always worry so much about that, dear boy. Just come as you are. These are serious theatre professionals. As soon as they see your work, they'll respect you."

He hung up and stood a little taller. His favorite teacher, favorite human, in fact, had that effect on him. Despite her encouragement to show up empty-handed, Craig spent all day Sunday baking impressive creations. He crafted cupcakes iced in the style of each character.

On Monday morning, he arrived at the college twenty minutes before seven. He always believed in being punctual and today was no exception. One by one, as the actors entered, he handed them their treat.

He'd also taken the liberty of going through the Pepperville Community College Yearbook, so he could put a face to every character.

"Darla, or should I call you Britney? "He handed a pink-frosted cupcake with frilly edges to the impeccably dressed young woman.

"Who are you? "She barked.

"I'm...um...Tony."

Her face softened and she took the cupcake from him. "Oh, okay. We're doing that, "she sniffed. "I'm not into the 'join hands and sing together' part of theater. I'm going to Hollywood soon and none of these people are getting in my way."

She glanced down at the tediously detailed cupcake he'd handed her. "As for this, I only eat once every other day. So, on Tuesday, I'll taste the frosting. "She continued on until she reached the other side of the stage, where yellow lockers lined the wall. She placed her things in three lockers and turned abruptly, dismayed that Craig was still staring at her. "What?"

He turned his attention to the other actors as quickly as possible. Britney would require a delicate touch. "She's going to love me by the end of this production," he uttered under his breath. "No matter what it takes."

"Sorry, bud. Were you talking to me?"

It was the third lead, Tate Williams. His body was compact and firm, the type of young man who won every athletic event he'd ever entered. Craig handed him the green frosted cake with tiny shoes on top.

He tried a different tact this time. "I baked cupcakes for everyone, to celebrate our first day. Yours is green because your character is dressed in khakis. Also, the shoes are significant because you lose them in the first act. I hope you're okay with that. Not the shoes, but your cupcake."

Craig held his breath, waiting for another negative response.

"Aww. This is really nice of you, man!!"Tate took the entire cupcake and placed it in his mouth. "What's your name, buddy? "He asked, as crumbs spewed onto the floor between them.

"I'm Craig, your third. You, me and Britney are the leads."

"Okay! Wow, I've never seen you around before. Were you new last semester?"

Craig blushed and hated himself for doing so. "You could say that."

He wondered if Tate knew he was only a senior in high school, if he'd be as receptive.

"Is this your first production, Tate? "Craig glanced around nervously, wondering if anyone else might have figured out he wasn't their age. No one seemed to care and he breathed a sigh of relief.

"It's my third. "Tate wiped the green frosting on his sleeve of his letter jacket. "I did the musical last year and then the Shakespeare Festival in October." He grinned. "Okay, now it's coming to me. You were Hercules, right? I thought I remembered you. You got a hole in your tights and I helped you duct tape them together."

Craig gulped. "No, not me."

There was a loud chatter that diverted their attention as other actors walked in en masse.

"I'll see you later, buddy!" Tate said, waving cheerfully as he jogged off.

The chorus made up the other cast, since the story took place out at sea with just three actors. Craig thought of them too, piping a musical note on top of their cupcakes. He left a note beside the box so they could all take one, deciding his time would be better spent trying to make nice with Britney.

When Ms. Bogart arrived, her hair tied up in a kerchief and her makeup impeccable, the entire room erupted into applause. At first, Craig wondered if they were doing it facetiously. After all, she was just a high school theatre teacher.

He reminded himself he was in the big leagues now; professionals didn't sink to the levels of high immature high school students.

"Thank you, thank you for your warm welcome."

She smiled, winking at Craig when she caught his eye. "I see some familiar faces from my high school productions, as well as some new ones. We'll get into introductions soon, but for now, I'd like to do some stretches."

By the second week of rehearsals, the cast had begun to gel. That's when their real personalities emerged, for better or for worse. In his sophomore year fall production of, *Git it, Got it Good*, Annabelle Fudge displayed a level of ease that left the rest of the cast reeling.

She brought homemade sausage, raw garlic and limburger cheese, staples in her family home. "I wasn't sure if I should, but you all are so nice, I don't have to be ashamed," she explained when someone ventured to ask what she ate every night.

It didn't take long for the entire theatre to absorb this overwhelming aroma. On opening night, one-third of the audience left at intermission, overcome by the distasteful scent.

Britney's true personality, not so much hidden on the first day as tempered, reached its full, raging potential by week two. She snapped at those who stumbled over their lines and made fun of mispronounced words.

"That's im-uh-jeen, Kendra, not I'm-a-gine," she said in a condescending tone. "You're old enough to figure that out. This isn't a high school production."

A smattering of uneasy giggles passed through the room. Ms. Bogart, seemingly enamored of Britney, said nothing.

One thing Craig learned from another actor was that Britney spent the first few weeks of every production criticizing everyone before she found her mark. Once she zeroed in on the person whose life would become nothing but misery for the duration of the production, she was relentless.

One day, as they finished rehearsals, Britney stuck a

polished fingernail in the air and motioned for Craig to join her. This was going to be the moment they made friends. Maybe she'd enjoyed his baking so much on the first day that she wanted more? He'd given up on trying to memorize her eating schedule, as others had done to track her moods.

"Hi Britt!" He said enthusiastically. "I'm on my way to the park for a little sun. Care to join me?"

Her face was twisted in what he assumed was pain. "Is there something wrong?" he asked innocently, touching her arm.

She jerked her arm away from him, nearly elbowing Craig in the face.

"Don't you EVER call me 'Britt' again."

As if on cue, the entire room emptied. There was only Craig and Britney; one carrying a rage that filled up every nook and cranny in the rehearsal space.

Since Craig had endured harsh words all through high school, it came as a shock to him when he felt his knees trembling.

"The reason I even speak to you off stage is that you need help with your acting."

"Oh? "He braced himself for whatever came next.

"To put it nicely, you stink. I don't know why Ms. Bogart—Clarice—would cast someone as weak as you in a lead role, but your understudy is just as awful."

Britney gestured toward Brian Finley, a mousy freshmen who lingered just outside the doorway.

"My father is recording this performance. It will be included on my reel, along with my head shots. While my acting is sublime, I realize there are others vying for roles who may be—"She paused for a dramatic intake of air before continuing. "Adequate. All this is to say, don't blow it for me!" She poked his chest with a pointed nail.

"I'll be watching your every move, Crudland. Every. Single. Move."

She flipped her hair behind her shoulder and turned away all in one motion.

While hurt by her thoughts on his acting, he was genuinely curious what she found so appalling. He decided it would have to wait for another day and nodded politely before exiting the room. The rest of the cast stared at him as he left, whether out of pity or admiration, he wasn't sure.

From that day on, Craig dreaded rehearsals. Britney was focused on making them as difficult for him as possible. Each time she corrected him, giggled at his acting, or shoved him, Ms. Bogart purposely diverted her gaze to someone else. *Had this all been her goal from the beginning?* To show him there wasn't anywhere he could feel safe? How could the one person he adored allow this to happen?

Meanwhile, Britney displayed her amazing memorization skills. She'd learned every single line and corrected everyone, mostly Craig, when they made the tiniest mistake.

"Don't mess around memorizing your lines, Craig," Tate cautioned. "Britney learns them all and she'll call you out if you screw up, even one word."

"That's 'drown,' not 'die,' Tate," Britney told him that day.

"Sorry, B. I had a late night at work. It won't happen again."

Tate glanced at Craig and nodded.

Craig split his astonished gaze between the two of them. How did she have this kind of control over people? Was she putting something in their drinks?

He started marking the days off his *Cats* calendar, covering each paw print-shape day in black when it was finished. He was of strong Shiardy stock, as his mother reminded him when he complained about carrying groceries fifteen steps up to their apartment.

On Friday of the following week, something completely unexpected happened.

Craig was in the bathroom, trying to regain control of his temper. They'd been rehearsing the scene where the shipmates were rescued by an intuitive songbird, whose song guided them to shore. After two days of rowing, Tate pulled the tattered boat ashore. His line was, "thanks for not eating me, man."

Every time he started to speak, Britney mumbled under her breath, "because you'd taste like failure."

By the fourth take, he'd had enough. "What's your problem?" he snapped, bringing the entire production to a screeching halt. Tate was the most pleasant member of the cast and the only one who hadn't melted down over Britney's insults.

She looked at him innocently. "I don't know what you're talking about!"

Ms. Bogart walked over to the stage and motioned for Craig to hop out of the boat and meet her. He fully expected that this time, she would ask him to be the peacemaker, because she knew Britney was a handful. Instead, she whispered, "why don't you go to the bathroom and collect yourself? Your energy is off and I think it's causing Britney to lash out at everyone."

Stunned, he stormed off in tears, more for the betrayal he felt from his teacher than anything Britney had done.

<h1>Act Two</h1>

While he was drying his eyes, someone came out of the stall. He was tall with dark hair and dark eyes, and when he smiled the room brightened.

"You having a rough day? I had one yesterday," he asked with concern, while washing his hands. "I'm Kel."

Craig wiped his face with the rough paper towel, reminding himself that tonight would require a seaweed facial and a steam. "I'm Craig. I don't usually lose control of my emotions."

Kel shrugged. "I get it. I've got someone in my life who makes me miserable four days out of five. But on that fifth day–"

The door opened and Tate stuck his head in. "Ms. Bogart sent me to check on you. Is everything good?"

Craig nodded.

"Okay then, you're needed on stage."

Craig pivoted back to Kel and shook his hand. "Thanks for understanding."

"Yeah, see ya around!" Kel said as Craig walked into the hallway. It was nice to know that not everyone in college was a Britney.

Rehearsals continued to be almost unbearable. If he didn't watch himself as he left the stage, Britney would be there with her foot out, ready to bring him down. It wasn't her nastiness that upset him the most, sadly he found more times than not people mistreated him. It was the fact that he expected everyone at this level to be more professional.

Ms. Bogart was curiously out of touch with the drama happening onstage. Britney's frequent outbursts were followed by, "let's take that again from the top of the page."

The few times Craig found the courage to speak with her, she'd waved him off with, "this isn't high school, Craig. I warned you."

The only joy for Craig was Kel. After their first meeting in the men's room, they'd bumped into each other again. Kel was taking summer classes at the college and always seemed to be around when Craig was rehearsing. The third time they met outside the cafeteria, Kel asked if Craig wanted help running lines. "I used to be in theatre and I miss it. It would be more for me than you."

Craig pushed aside his lingering doubts. Not everyone in the world was cruel, he reminded himself. "Okay. As long as you don't need to get to class."

Kel looked at his watch. "No, I've got an hour."

They ran lines over lunch every day for the next two weeks. Kel had amazing timing. "You should audition in New York," Craig encouraged.

"Nah. I'm gonna work in my dad's vacuum repair shop as soon as I finish school. Nobody leaves town, and I don't want to be the first. Maybe they don't let you come back! What would I do if I couldn't have some of my mom's boysenberry pie at Thanksgiving?"

Craig never considered that there were people who liked their families. He tolerated his mother and his half-sister, but not enough to stick around if he had a way out.

"You know, you're a cool guy. When I was in high school, I wasn't half as mature."

Kel continued munching on his double order of cheese fries, as if he hadn't just spilled Craig's big secret.

"What? How did you..."

"I looked for your picture in the yearbook and didn't find it. That's when I picked up my kid brother's yearbook, and bam!" He slammed his palm on the table, causing everyone in the cafeteria to stare at them in unison. "There you were."

Craig glanced around nervously. Once everyone else had gone back to their conversations, he leaned in close to Kel. "Please don't tell anyone!" He begged.

"Why not? Nobody cares about that. Heck, there are people the same age as my dad in some of my classes. This is community college, not high school."

"Miss Powertrip does. "Craig gave all of the actors alternate names, so he didn't have to worry if they were Kel's friends or not when they were speaking. "She'll take it as a sign of weakness."

"That makes sense," Kel replied. "Your secret is safe with me." He scooted the fry basket over to Craig and they sat in silence, sharing fries for the rest of their lunch hour.

The next morning at rehearsal, Ms. Bogart remarked, "Craig, you've really turned a corner. I see great things in your future."

He stood a little taller and allowed himself a brief glance in Britney's direction. She shook her head, but for once, didn't disagree. This momentary cease fire didn't stop her from stepping on his lines twice during dress rehearsal. Both times she smiled her sickly sweet smile and shrugged her shoulders. It was maddening.

Finally, it was dress rehearsal week. They'd perform all the way through for three nights and then would have four performances in a row. Under normal circumstances, it was demanding and exhausting. With Britney's tension permeating the room, it was almost intolerable.

The cast, with the exception of Tate, stopped speaking to Craig. He realized immediately that this was another attempt by Britney to sabotage his performance.

"Why do you want me to fail so badly?" Craig asked after the first dress rehearsal. "If I mess up tomorrow night, it's going to make your audition tape look sloppy."

"Oh, Crudland," she teased in a singsong voice. "You don't understand the world at all. When it became apparent you weren't up to the task of a lead role, I changed my plan."

She smiled, bright-pink lipstick visible on her top teeth. "The more you screw up, the more I'll swoop in, ad-libbing lines to make up for your mistakes. I'm going to come out of this smelling like a rose either way."

Craig had no recourse but to walk away. No one stood up to Britney, most of all, his formerly-favorite teacher. He couldn't wait until he saw Kel again. Kel was the only person in his corner. At least he had one ally.

That day, he poured out his soul. For the first time in his life, he felt calm.

"This person--your Miss Powertrip--is nasty. It's clear she's never going to change. Get through the next two weekends, plus matinees and you'll never have to talk to her again."

Act Three

Craig nodded through tears of joy. Someone finally understood his pain. "What should I do? I'm afraid she'll ruin our performances and everyone will blame me."

Kel sucked the sides of his mouth in so that they

touched. Craig discovered early on that this was his body language for thinking things over.

"Well, you could beat her to the punch and step on *her* lines. But she would find a way to get revenge and it would never end. Or..."

"Or?"

"Tonight, because it's opening night, you need to show up while she's getting her makeup done. Stand there, using your best horror movie face, without saying a word. Eventually she's going to get the hint that you need to talk to her alone. I'm sure she'll be curious why you're doing that. That's when you tell her in no uncertain terms that you know her secret and you'll tell everyone if she messes with you."

Craig's eyes widened. "I don't have any idea what her secret is. How would I find out?"

Kel shook his head and smiled. "You don't need to. Everyone has a big secret. People who are mean like that carry the biggest ones. That's why they have to lash out first."

He thought about it. The idea was simple, but so was Britney. All through rehearsals she'd been as cruel as every single kid in his grade put together. If he could summon the courage to put her in her place now, maybe she would think twice the next time.

"Okay, I'll do it. We can talk tomorrow and I'll let you know how it goes. Oh, Kel—are you coming tonight?"

Kel grinned from ear to ear. "Are you kidding? I

wouldn't miss the big performance. Yours on stage and off!"

That evening, Craig sat patiently as the hair and makeup group worked on him. They came up with an ingenious idea to use Dippity Do, a green hair gel of industrial strength, to style his hair as though he'd been lost at sea in raging winds. They also glued clear glass gems onto his cheeks to simulate water droplets. His clothing was torn and dampened right before the performance.

Craig looked in the mirror feeling confident he was ready to confront Britney, or Darla, her character. Both were equally reprehensible.

He walked up to her dressing room, which doubled as a janitor's closet but was the only actual private space used as a dressing room, and knocked on the door.

One of the many extras who followed Britney around opened the door and glared at him. "What? We're busy in here."

Craig peeked around her, where lights hung from the ceiling attached to extension cords. In the center of the closet, Britney sat on a tall chair while her makeup was applied.

"Oh, it's little rodent," she cooed facetiously. "Come in, I need to speak with you."

The extra walked outside of the closet, allowing enough space for Craig to enter.

"I just want you to know, despite the fact that your acting is subpar, I may find time to tutor you next summer. I'll be home on a break from auditions. Forty dollars an hour, no discounts." She turned her head to one side and then the other, admiring the enormous stack of blonde hair that had been teased and sprayed at least a foot taller than Britney.

"That's only if I don't have other offers," she continued.

Craig gulped. "Thank you, Britney. But I wanted to talk to you as well. It's about a secret of–"

"Babe! You came!" Her voice took on a syrupy quality Craig hadn't experienced before. It was almost more distasteful than her regular snickers. He pivoted around, where a large bouquet of flowers hid another human.

"Rodent, take my flowers and put them in water," Britney commanded.

His plan unraveling quickly, Craig took the bouquet. He'd just dump them in the trash. That would show her. When he saw the face behind the flowers, his knees shook.

"Kel?"

"Craig?"

"This is the person you–"

There was an awkward silence.

"Leave now, Crudland. My flowers need water and my boyfriend needs to shower me with adoring words!" Britney snapped.

Craig rushed out of the closet, well aware of the damage he'd do to his makeup if he allowed his emotions to take control.

"Craig! Wait!"

He couldn't face Kel. Another betrayal. "No, you've been playing me all along. I should have known. Nobody in this world gets me."

Kel grabbed his arm, causing him to turn.

"I didn't know, honest. The fact that she's been treating you like this shocks me. She's really a good person, once you get past the crusty surface."

Craig stared into Kel's eyes, unsure if what he saw was honesty or embarrassment at having been caught, or maybe a little bit of both. "I have a show to prepare for. Who knows how badly she'll embarrass me tonight? Oh, and this ridiculously big bouquet needs water."

He paused momentarily, hoping Kel would admit to his crimes. When no such confession was forthcoming, he continued, "I'm sorry I trusted you," he said firmly as he walked away. It was the most challenging role he'd ever played: scorned friend caught in a web of lies while putting on the best performance of his acting career. It wouldn't fit on a resume, but it certainly gave his acting a new level of professionalism.

During act one, Britney tried tripping him once but instead caught her toe on an oar inside the boat. When she fell over, the audience gasped. Jumping to her feet quickly, she cried, "I'm going to make it. I haven't eaten in days and I can barely stand, but Darla Donovan never gives up!"

In the second half of act two, Craig paused during his soliloquy about how he had regrets in his life.

When Britney attempted to jump in, he interrupted her, finishing his speech flawlessly. The only person who was going to make a fool of themselves on her audition tape was Britney herself.

As they neared the end of the performance, clearly frustrated with her night, she gave Craig a big shove as he exited the boat. He fell forward into an unsuspecting Tate.

Their eyes met for a moment as Craig panicked, forgetting next line. It was at that moment that Tate delivered perhaps the best ad-lib Craig would experience in his entire life. He would go on to share it with his theatre students for the rest of his career.

"I've got you, little buddy. We're connected now and forever."

The audience gasped and clapped enthusiastically.

After they took their bow and a second curtain call, the cast came over and congratulated Craig. No longer fearful of Britney, they heaped praise on him. It was time.

Wearing the blush of victory, Craig walked up to Britney, who was nursing her wounds with Kel.

"Nice work, Britt." He said with sarcasm dripping from his voice. "Oh, I wanted you to know before tomorrow's matinee, I know your secret."

"What? "She looked up in surprise, and then over to her boyfriend. "Did you tell him?"

"No! I wouldn't!" Kel's face was beet red. "Really! I wouldn't!"

Britney jumped off her chair and rushed out of the room, leaving Kel and Craig alone.

"If I knew it was Britney, I never would have suggested–"

"Now that you know it's her, does that make what she did to me okay?"

There wasn't a response forthcoming, so Craig decided it was time to go. He had a cast party and new friends to enjoy.

"Craig! Wait!" Kel grabbed his arm from behind. Craig shook it loose and continued walking. He felt a touch on his arm again, this time, much softer.

"Craig? May I have a word?"

It was Ms. Bogart.

"I guess." He no longer looked to her for approval. She'd disappointed him more than once. The biggest lesson he'd learned this summer was never to put anyone on a pedestal.

"Craig, Britney came to me with concerns that you were bullying her."

His mouth dropped open.

"Haven't you been paying attention? This entire production she's done nothing but make my life miserable! Mine and the rest of the cast!"

"I know," she said quietly. "Can we go into the choir room so we won't be interrupted?"

Using every ounce of kindness he had left in his body, he nodded and followed her.

I t had been three months since *Row Your Way to Happiness* closed.

The local daily paper, published Sundays,

Wednesdays and every-other Friday, gave a glowing review of Craig's performance. "Craiglund Shiardy's performance as Tony was an emotional connection to the audience we'd never felt before. Pepperville Junior College has a true gem in Mr. Shiardy."

Even his stepfather showed up for the final performance. That night, he and Britney held hands as they took their final bow. "I'll let you know when I get my first job, okay?" She said, kissing him on the cheek.

"Please do," Craig replied. It was all an act, but it was no longer an act that frightened him.

Kel took her arm and escorted Britney to the lobby, where her adoring fans awaited her. Craig wasn't ready to forgive Kel, even though he'd reached out many times.

The air turned crisp and school began again, much to his dismay. Craig was surprised when he was greeted with cheers his first day. "Didn't know you had it in you, man," one of his chief tormentors said as he punched him playfully in the arm. Apparently, all it took to bring a bully to his senses was to have a write-up in the local paper.

Though there were still those who giggled and openly made fun of him, senior year was going much better than he'd anticipated.

Every Tuesday, he stopped on Plum Street before going home. By now, he'd been given a key.

"Are you decent, Clarice? He knocked lightly before opening the door.

"No, never!" she chuckled.

Craig handed her hot cross buns, this week's creation.

"Do you have time to sit for a minute?"

"I have all the time, honey," he replied. "My mom is making her meatloaf tonight."

Craig flopped down in the brown couch. "What's new with Britney?"

Clarice rolled her eyes and sat back in her chair. "Same old. I wish I could say she's decided to leave, but there's always a reason she can't go. She started beauty school, you know."

"I do know." Craig patted the back of his head absently. "I got the Britney special last week. It feels a little crooked, but I'll live."

"I just wanted to thank you again, for keeping our secret," his favorite person in the world said.

That evening after the performance, he was shocked by her words. He no longer felt animosity toward Ms. Bogart, only compassion. They became fast friends from that moment on, bonding over shared emotions of loneliness and fear. The most important lesson he learned that night: the idea of a secret is the most powerful weapon a person can possess.

Craig,

Britney says you know. I don't understand who told you, but we must never make it public. It would ruin both of our lives if it got out that I'm her mother. I was a foolish teen and her father was my theater teacher. It's better that she grew up as my cousin's child, don't you think? I promise, I'll make sure she treats you better from now on. You've always been my favorite student.

Read Franniebell and Purple Wonder now!

About the Author

USA TODAY Bestselling Author, Joann Keder raised a family and taught piano lessons on the Great Plains of Nebraska, all the while secretly dreaming of a career as a writer.

At the age of 35 she timidly took her first college course, unsure if she had what it took to go much further. At the age of 42 she received her Masters Degree in Creative Writing, creating her first novella, *The Something That Happened in Pepperville* as her thesis.

An abrupt move to the Pacific Northwest and much personal trauma lead to a re-examination of who and what she was meant to be.

Today, her passions include hiking, writing and chocolate, not necessarily in that order.

Find Joann on social media:

Also by Joann Keder

Pepperville Stories

The Story of Keilah

Secrets and Sunflowers

Franniebell and Purple Wonder

Piney Falls Mysteries

Welcome to Piney Falls

Saving Piper Moonlight

Tales of Naybor Manor

Lavender's Tangled Tree

The Twisted Stitch Society

Charming Mysteries

Oceanberry Blues

Tangerine Troubles

Perilously Pink

Emory Bing Mysteries

Ebook only

Be the first to hear about new releases! Sign up for my newsletter here:

http://www.joannkeder.com

www.ingramcontent.com/pod-product-compliance
Lightning Source LLC
Chambersburg PA
CBHW051257210726
48287CB00002B/539